# A Narcissistic Kind Of Love

Short stories of loving, surviving, and recovering from narcissistic relationships.

AG Narratives

The names of the individuals have been changed to protect their identities.

**Trigger warning:** The stories that follow may range from disturbing to severe, including instances of violence and even legal consequences for those involved. Narcissistic abuse is real. Recognizing the signs is the first step toward awareness, protection, and healing.

✝

*"Let's not mistake the lack of empathy with stoicism."*

✝

*"You have power over your mind, not outside events. Realize this and you will have strength."*

**– Marcus Aurelius.**

✝

# Author's Note

Many people who have endured or are currently enduring narcissistic abuse often carry a heavy burden of self-blame. I have heard it time and again: *"I should've known better."* But the truth is, this kind of abuse distorts your reality. It breeds self-doubt, insecurity, and a loneliness that you may have never experienced before. You begin to second-guess and even third guess your decisions, which can make you feel like you have played a part and should have walked away long ago. That regret can feel like a heavy weight you drag around daily.

But here's the truth: the experience doesn't define you. It is not your weakness; it reveals your strength. What you went through is teaching you to evolve into a more powerful, self-aware version of yourself. One who now recognizes that not everyone is worthy of access to your life. One who refuses to shrink themselves just to fit into someone else's small world.

The lesson? Stand tall. Be firm. Never doubt your intuition. Protect what is sacred in you, especially the parts that were once overlooked and ignored.

Knowing your worth is not optional, it is essential. You are the one person who deserves all of you. Your boundaries are sacred ground, not a playground for toxic behavior.

Healing is not a switch you can just turn on; it is a process that takes intentional work. Learning to separate the person from the lesson and reflecting on what initially drew you in can help you reclaim inner peace. It is how you begin to forgive yourself, and eventually, move forward.

If you feel stuck or "trapped," please know this: therapy can help. So can community surround yourself with trusted friends and family. These connections are vital to your mental and emotional well-being.

And one simple, powerful practice. Look at yourself in the mirror for five minutes each day without any words. It may feel small now, but one day, you will thank yourself for showing up even when it was hard.

†

# Contents

# Echoes of the Heart

E.J. sat alone in the apartment he once shared with Marletta, the silence so full it felt like another person in the room. The early morning light crept through the blinds, casting slatted shadows across the floor, like prison bars he no longer needed to imagine. It had been two months since she left, and still, every corner echoed with her voice, every mirror still whispered with her laughter.

They had been together for three years. Three years of smiles that never quite reached her eyes, apologies that came with conditions, love that demanded an invisible tax he was too blind to audit until it was too late.

He remembered the first time he saw her, at a friend's party. She had that kind of allure that stops time, not just beauty in the classic sense, but charisma, magnetism. When she spoke to him, it was as if a spotlight shone on his existence for the first time. She asked questions like she genuinely cared about the answers. In hindsight, he realized she was memorizing, not understanding. Everything he said became data. Usable. Weaponizable.

"You're so emotionally intelligent," she had said once during their second month together. "Most men are not. You are special, EJ."

He did not know then that her compliments were currency for loyalty, his loyalty. The praise came fast and warm, a flood that washed away his self-doubt, his boundaries, his caution. He became addicted to her approval, chasing it like a drug even when it turned scarce.

By the six-month mark, things began to change imperceptibly at first. She criticized how he spoke, how he dressed, and who his friends were. "I'm only telling you this because I care," she would say, her tone laced with condescension, "You deserve to be your best self."

He began doubting himself. His world grew smaller. His once colorful life, a tapestry of friendships, hobbies, and dreams, dulled into greyscale. He stopped seeing his friends, too tired to argue with her subtle disapproval. He quit his side photography gigs because they "took time away from us." In truth, it took time away from her control.

And then came the gaslighting.

"I never said that" she would insist, her eyes wide with mock hurt. "You're remembering it wrong."

EJ learned to distrust his memory, his instincts. He apologized for things he did not do. He made excuses for her behavior to friends who dared to point out the red flags. "She's just passionate," he would say. "She had a rough childhood. She needs patience."

In truth, she needed submission.

The worst was the way she rewrote reality. If he cried, he was "too sensitive." If he showed anger, he was "abusive." If he tried to set a boundary, he was "controlling." She accused him of the very things she did, using projection as both shield and sword.

Still, he stayed. Why?

Because she had convinced him he was broken. That without her, no one would love him. That she alone saw the real him, the flawed treasure that others would discard. And he believed it.

The first time he caught her lying about where she had been, he confronted her. She turned it around. "You are stalking me? Don't you trust me? You are the manipulative one." And he believed that, too.

When she cheated, it was his fault. "You were distant," she claimed. "You don't make me feel wanted."

So, he gave more. Loved harder. Made himself smaller.

Until there was nothing left of him.

The breakup was not explosive. It was surgical. Cold. One morning, she simply announced, "I think we've outgrown each other." No tears. No regret. She had already replaced him with someone newer, more useful.

EJ did not fight it this time. He had no strength left. He merely nodded and watched her pack. She did not even take all her things. She left behind a sweater, some books, and a perfume bottle. Tiny landmines.

The weeks after, he replayed everything. Every word. Every fight. Every moment he felt off but said nothing. He thought about how he had abandoned his friends, lost touch with family, and sidelined his dreams. For what?

Love?

Or the idea of it?

He felt it was his fault. Not because it truly was, but because he had been conditioned to believe so. That was her masterpiece. Her greatest con. She had not just manipulated him; she taught him to manipulate himself.

Therapy helped. Slowly.

"You were in a trauma bond," his therapist explained. "Narcissistic abuse cycles through idealization, devaluation, and discard. You were groomed to depend on her."

He hated that word, groomed. It made him feel weak. Naive. But it was the truth. A painful, liberating truth.

He started journaling. Not for clarity at first, but out of necessity. His head felt like a broken record, looping old arguments, rehearsing what he should have said, fantasizing about closure that would never come.

"I let it happen," he wrote once. "Why didn't I leave sooner?"

His therapist replied, "Because you were surviving. That is not weakness, it is strategy. You did what you had to do to cope."

Little by little, he reclaimed his time. Reached out to old friends. Took long walks. Picked up his camera again. The lens became his new way of seeing, reframing the world, including himself.

The guilt did not vanish, but it changed. From self-blame to grief. Grief for the years lost, the parts of himself abandoned, the illusions shattered.

And then one day, standing in the golden hour light, capturing a child laughing in a park, Elliot felt something he had not in years.

Hope.

Not a grand, cinematic hope. But a quiet one. A whisper. A promise that he could build something new, not despite the pain, but through it.

He looked at the photograph he had just taken. It was imperfect. Slightly out of focus. Real.

And he smiled. It was that moment he felt he was going to be ok.

✝

# Nanie's Process of why she kept going back:

The pull of disappointing love was one Nanie knew of. At least, that is what she told herself every time she walked away from him again. She would sit in the quiet, sometimes in her car, sometimes on the edge of her bed, breathing slowly through the lump in her throat, knowing deep down that she deserved more. More consistency. More love. More respect. But somehow, days or weeks later, she would find herself right back where she swore, she would never return. answering his texts, picking up his late-night calls, letting him back into the fragile corners of her heart.

It was not just about him. It was about her, the woman who kept forgiving, kept waiting, kept hoping that maybe this time, he would be different. That *they* would be different.

## Her Illusion of Potential

From the beginning, their connection felt electric, instant, and undeniable. He had a charm about him that made her feel seen, like she was the only one in the room. He said all the right things at first, asked her about her dreams, remembered her favorite tea, and made her laugh when her world felt heavy.

But it did not take long for the cracks to appear. He canceled plans at last minute. Messages left unread. Promises, big and small never kept. And every time Nanie asked for more, he gave her just enough to keep her hanging on. A thoughtful message. A short apology. A weekend where he seemed all in.

She clung to those moments. They were rare, but they were real in her mind. Weren't they? They had to be. She did not imagine the tenderness in his voice when he said he cared. She did not fabricate the way his eyes softened when he told her she mattered. But those fleeting moments stood in sharp contrast to the long stretches of emotional absence and confusion.

She did not fall in love with the man he was. She fell in love with the man he *could* be. The version of him he showed in glimpses, the kind, attentive, emotionally present version was the one she kept chasing. The one she needed him to be. Turns out potential is a powerful drug.

## Her Emotional Familiarity

There was something else. Something deeper and harder to name. The way he made her feel, anxious, uncertain, hopeful and then crushed felt oddly familiar. It mimicked relationships she had experienced before, maybe even in childhood. The sense that love was something to be earned, to fight for. That if she just did enough, stayed long enough, proved her worth she would be chosen, finally and fully.

This emotional pattern, though painful, gave her a strange sense of comfort. Not because it was good, but because it was known. And humans, by nature, tend to return to what feels familiar even when it hurts. Especially when it hurts.

So, she stayed. Not all at once. Not blindly. She left many times, told her friends she was done, cried herself to sleep after blocking his number. But every time he came back with a half-apology and that look in his eyes, she found herself slowly folding. She mistook *his* need for *her* as love. And, in some twisted way, it was their love, just the broken kind.

## Her Hope for Change

Hope can be a beautiful thing. But in the wrong context, it can also be dangerous. Nanie hoped he would change. Hoped he would grow. Hoped one day he would wake up and realize she was everything he ever wanted, and he would never risk losing her again.

She saw his wounds, the parts of him that were still healing. He was not heartless. He was human, inconsistent, insecure, sometimes lost. And she believed in healing. She believed that love could be the thing that helped him grow.

So, she gave. And gave. And gave.

But the truth was, he was not trying. Not really. He liked having her there. He liked knowing she would always pick up, always come back. But liking her was different from loving her. And wanting her in his life was different from choosing her fully, consistently, without games or gaps.

Still, Nanie held on. Because letting go would mean admitting that the story she had written in her head, the future she envisioned with him was not real. And grief, even of a dream, is hard to face.

## Her Fear of Starting Over

There is a unique loneliness that comes with walking away from someone who still has a piece of your heart. Nanie was not just afraid of losing him, she was afraid of starting over. The thought of opening to someone new, explaining her scars, building trust from scratch felt exhausting.

She had already invested so much. Time. Emotion. Forgiveness. She did not want it all to be for nothing.

So, she convinced herself that maybe if she just waited a little longer, things would finally shift. That love, *real* love, required patience and resilience. And maybe it does, but it also requires reciprocity. And that was the part she kept ignoring.

## The Lies We Tell Ourselves

"I'm strong enough to handle this."

"He's just going through a rough patch."

"It's not always bad."

"I know he loves me; he just doesn't know how to show it."

These were the mantras Nanie repeated to herself in the quiet moments, the in-between times when the relationship was neither fully alive nor fully dead. These rationalizations helped her cope. Helped her stay.

But over time, even she began to dislike the story. The weight of pretending grew heavy. The emotional toll showed in her eyes, in the way she smiled less, laughed quieter, second-guessed her worth more and more.

Deep down, she started to understand this was not love. At least not the kind that nourishes. It was love with sharp edges. Love that cost her peace. Love that always left her waiting.

## Letting Go is the Hardest Kind of Brave.

The real turning point did not come with a dramatic betrayal or a final fight. It came in a quiet moment of clarity. One night, Nanie sat on her porch, alone, wrapped in a blanket and the silence of knowing better. And for the first time, she did not reach for her phone. She did not check if he had texted. She did not plan what to say next time he came calling.

She just sat there and let the truth rise: *She had become someone she barely recognized in the process of trying to keep someone who never truly chose her.*

That is when she knew. It was time to stop hoping. Not because she did not believe in love anymore, but because she finally believed in herself.

Letting go was not a single moment. It was a series of choices to ignore his messages, to grieve what could have been, to rebuild her self-worth brick by brick. Some days, the loneliness roared louder than ever. But with every boundary she set, she became a little stronger. A little freer.

And eventually, Nanie found peace. Not the kind that came from someone else finally treating her right, but the kind that came from treating herself right.

## Her Final Reflection

Nanie did not go back to him because she was weak. She went back because she was human hopeful, hurting, trying. She wanted to believe that love could conquer all, that emotional investment guaranteed a return. But life does not work that way. Love must be mutual, not a prize won through sacrifice.

Her story is not one of foolishness, but of growth. Of learning the difference between connection and commitment. Between temporary comfort and lasting respect. Between someone who says the right things, and someone who shows up consistently, wholeheartedly, without question.

In the end, Nanie did not walk away from him. She walked toward herself.

✝

# Tina D.

Her body warned her long before her mind could catch up. Every call, every visit, every moment he stepped into her space sent her nervous system into chaos. Her anxiety would skyrocket. It was unlike anything she had experienced before, so she assumed something must be wrong with *her*. Maybe she was changing, becoming more sensitive, maybe it was just stress.

She tried to stay calm around him, but peace never came unless she had a drink or two. His energy was loud, unpredictable, and emotionally draining. Over time, she began blaming herself for everything. When movie nights turned sour, or nights out with friends ended in silence and arguments in the car. He would disappear for days, ignoring her calls and texts, while she twisted herself into knots trying to explain away misunderstandings he created.

Every time an event involved others—travel plans, holidays, social gatherings, he transformed into someone else. Someone colder. Distant. Hostile. She was exhausted and felt stuck. A heavy, dark energy hung over her. She was suffocating, depressed, and profoundly alone.

Even in her pain, whether it was a headache, period cramps, or the flu, he showed no empathy. He would quickly redirect the attention to himself, brushing her off with, "Stop it, I don't feel good either." If she struggled, he would watch blankly, then change the subject to something trivial he cared about.

She had never experienced anything like this. A man who was competing with her, constantly jealous, and quick to diminish her with laughter or a smirk. And when she confronted him? "Relax, I'm just playing."

They broke up multiple times. Each time, he returned in tears, full of apologies and promises to change. He was convincing, but his actions never aligned with his words. He would start grand gestures, planning trips or surprises, only to later blame others when things fell apart. He was always the victim; nothing was ever his fault.

He would cancel plans at the last minute or pick fights just before a trip, leaving her in a panic and begging him not to ruin it. She was constantly left explaining his behavior, his absences, and his mood swings to others. It was all a performance. for attention, for control.

In public, he was charming. In private, he was either a "project" to fix or a monster she could not recognize. He accused her of cheating without cause, sending her into emotional spirals just to prove her loyalty. He did not want a happy, healthy woman, he wanted to sabotage her spirit.

She kept believing there was a good man buried deep inside him. She covered for him, painted him in a better light to friends and family, even distancing herself from those who voiced concerns. The only time he showed affection was during sex, and even that became robotic, more punishment than passion. He would hold her down, bite her face, repeat the same lines, and ignore her when she said she did not like it. The more she spoke up, the more he would it. When she confronted his aggression, he would mock her: "Now was that better? Now you can stop complaining."

There was no warmth. No celebration. Only terror, large and small. Even during her proudest accomplishments, when others cheered her on, he was cold, dismissive, and bitter. It was clear he did not want to see her shine.

And yet, when she pulled away, he would unravel, staging hospital emergencies, crying on the phone, claiming he was dying without her. "I love you so much it's physically killing me," he would say. But his actions never reflected love. He was the architect of chaos, a master of illusion.

Now, four years later, she is still healing, still trying to reclaim the version of herself she lost in that relationship.

✝

*"No one plays the victim better than the person who caused the damage."*

✝

# Rodrick W.

The woman I spent nine years with was a love at first sight. I can be honest and say it was mostly physical attraction; she was striking, her fits were always on point, nails, hair, and makeup were flawless. She had everything going on her side that would stop men and women in their tracks, and getting to know her was like a beautiful thunderstorm because after the rains came clear skies and sunshine. Make-up sex was even better than our normal interaction. Sexually, we were animals in the wild. What more could a man ask for, right? Right, well, let me just start with what this man did not ask for. Five months into the relationship, I started to notice certain patterns. We would go out for a few drinks, and she would get flirtatious with other men. There was one time she suggested a place that later I realized was a gay lounge. She would be extremely flirtatious with gay couples only, which allowed me to see that she was doing all of it to create fights and comparisons. I talked to her about it a few times and asked her to chill on that, and how it looked and made me feel. She snapped off so bad it was scary. throwing things, calling me jealous and controlling, saying no man, not even her dad, could discipline her, so what made me think I could ever? She got up and stormed off and threw my favorite coffee cup I kept at her house at the mirror, the mirror, and the cup shattered on the floor and dresser. She turns around and walks back towards me in the glass and cuts her foot. Falling to the ground screaming. I jumped up, concerned, and tried to help. Her foot was bleeding, and she was screaming like a three-year-old who had just fallen off a bike. She started telling me to move, pushing my hands away, yelling "don't touch me! Leave me alone." I stood up and stepped back with both hands up, asking What can I do to help? "Nothing!!!!" I was hurt, she was hurting, and I was so in love with this woman that I started taking on her emotions. I felt bad for upsetting her and felt horrible that I was the cause of her pain. I stood there waiting for her to calm down while assessing her injury. Calmly walking over to the restroom for a towel. I kneel with the towel and place it on her foot, rubbing her back with my other arm. For a second, she was calming down until she jerked away from me and looked at me with anger and yelled. "GET OUT!" A still quite chilled throughout her building. Even a neighbor's light flickered on and off across the hallway. I stood up, looked at her, she was clearly upset, so I left. Being a tall, intimidating-looking black man, my dad taught me to always be aware of my surroundings and how to read others' responses around me. I wanted to be there for her while thinking of my safety. It was like she was performing for an audience, so I left. That night scared me so bad it was hard to go back, even picking up the phone to talk or text her was overwhelming and felt odd. I shared my experience with my parents, and they recommended that I leave her alone. It was what I wanted to hear; I needed some support to do what was on my heart to do. I never called her, and she never reached out until exactly a year after the incident which I thought was strange and asked if we could meet so, we met up for lunch. She apologized for what happen and started telling me, she was going through so much I was never aware of. She laid out her attempted suicide while we were together, the medication she was on since childhood for anxiety and depression because her father was abusive to her and her mom. My heart went out to her, and we started being friends. Taking things slow and learning each other again. New feelings were built, and we became tighter than before. After all I loved her. One summer, I went to her family reunion excited about building a life with her and becoming more supportive with her past experiences and traumas. The trip was going well and on the second day I met more family than the first day. Her close cousins that were like her siblings and finally had the opportunity to sit and eat with her mom. A woman just as beautiful as her daughter. By the third day, her mom approaches me while I was getting chairs out the car. She started telling me how happy she was that her daughter found a young man who was willing to accept her for who she was. I looked at her with confidence and proudly said "of *course, I love your daughter and here to support her in every way. I know she had a difficult childhood, and I want to make her feel safe.*" Her mom looks at me with one of the coldest looks I had ever seen and said "my daughter has had a great childhood. Her dad and I gave the best of what any parents could offer a child. I immediately apologized and started to explain what I meant but, before I could she comes running over, nervously yelling mom, mom. Uncle T, is looking for you. Instantly, that feeling from a year ago surfaced but I did not want to ruin the trip on her family reunion, so I decided to shake it off. We arrived back home, and I mentioned the incident and told her I hope her mom was not offended. I was only trying to express my love for her, and with the same cold, dirty look her mom gave me, she looked at me and said: "Rodrick, you are a stupid man. You believe anything anyone tells you because you are a FN looser. I was only kidding when I told you that. I don't know my father. He was killed in the army when I was 5 years old." she laughed out loud and said "I bet you also believe that shit. She continues to laugh saying" that is why I love you." and walks towards me for a kiss. I was stunned and speechless. I finally mustered up the words to say "what do you mean? What is going on with you!" She walked off to pour herself a drink and said trust me. You do not want to know." That night I declined her offer to stay over by telling her my mom needed me to pick up something and went home. Reflecting all night and too embarrassed to share it with family and friends I took the cowardly way out and avoided her with excuse after excuse for the next few days. Deciding to man up on day four, I called her to talk about the odd behavior and how uncomfortable I was with her making up horrible lies of that magnitude. She answered the phone and immediately said "let me call you right back." Right back, never came so I picked up the phone and called her back. I went straight to voicemail for the next few days until I finally processed the fact she had blocked me. I guess, I was stupid. I never heard from her again but, whatever was going on with her, I can't help but feel I seen it already in her mom's eyes.

# Lauren

A decade of dating a monster disguised as a prince almost destroyed Lauren. Early in the relationship, James was confident, charismatic, and affectionate. he would do anything to shower her with love and attention. He appeared to be committed to building a lifelong structure. He spoke so spiritually. Bringing God into every conversation. How he prayed for her, asking God for a beautiful, strong woman. He often compared her to the women in his life who raised him and attributed that to why he was the great man that he was. Their first date had all the chivalrous components she was accustomed to in a man and thought nothing of it. opening doors, paying for the meal, and refusing her money, allowing her to speak, and showing his undivided attention, the subtle yet nervous looks at her beauty. Checking out her hair, nails, skin, and random compliments just to see her blush. James was not Laurens' physical type, but everything he showed her in the beginning checked all her boxes, and that was enough for her. She was tired of being single. And wanted to share her life with someone willing to put in an effort to build something special.

60 days into the relationship, sex was introduced, and that is when she started to notice subtle red flags. Slightly intense, but she found them thrilling, overly aggressive and controlling in bed. Some of his sex talks were concerning, but she always excused it for the passionate, heated, and excellent connection they had in bed. Sex brought out a needy James, who had to know her every move. If he called and she did not pick up, he would question her whereabouts and the reason she did not answer. His delivery on how many times

he called, and how she must have seen them. His voice would elevate, talking over her, and when she expressed how she did not appreciate how he was talking to her, it was always downplayed with an excuse. Like how he worked in a loud environment, needing to speak loudly, and she was overreacting, she needed to relax. He apologized when he wanted her to stop correcting him and would turn around and repeat the same behavior the next time she missed his calls.

His controlling nature tightened when he felt she was pulling away; he would book a vacation, become clingier, reminding her she was all he had, needed, and could not live without. Sex was the main thing he used to control her. He loved the responses he caused, and it was the only time he was sure she was in total submission to him. His sex talk became increasingly aggressive in the heat of it he would say things like "you better not ever leave me." You belong to me and no one else. Do you hear me? Say yes," if she did not answer, he would do uncomfortable things he knew she did not like until she pushed him away, and that would cause an argument. The cycle was always the same. She ended up being the problem. Lauren felt like she was never heard, or taken seriously, and tried to leave him several times and round it goes. He reacts manipulatively; apologies, sex, better sex, and gaslighting that some how escalated into threats. He had to keep her emotionally dependent. He would confuse her with his actions and implied violence by punch walls, verbal threats but never what he considered "over the line" yet

He would beg for forgiveness, lace in blame. Never taking accountability and using her strengths to weaken her mind. Things were spiraling out of control fast for Lauren, the woman she was, was slowly declining. She became more dependent on the dysfunction out of fear. She saw in him a severely unstable individual who was extremely unpredictable and emotionally unhinged. No one around them, friends, or family knew this was a reality. Her silence was paralyzing her, the realization was overwhelming and where would she even start to tell her story. No one would believe her because the outside was a perfect couple. She had become her abuser. Manipulating the world with smiles, laughs, and reassurance if someone suspected anything. Protecting him because it felt like an attack on her. She confused the pain of breakups as a sign that they were meant to be together, and not the trauma her mind and body were trying to recover from, and the moment she reached a pivotal point in a week-long separation, he would appear, smothering her with tears, gifts and everything she needed to hear to make the heartaches go away. Months of highs until he became bored with himself and brought in his weeks of lows and drama-filled chaos. Physically, she was a mess. Her hair started thinning, her skin was always dry and sensitive, she was getting sick often and calling off work. In her time of needing some TLC were opportunities for him to shame her for not going to work. Ignoring getting her a glass of water and medicine. On many occasions, she had just lay in bed crying. Holding on to false hopes of his support and affection that he was never going to give. One day he walked in on her getting out of the shower and made a comment about her losing a lot of weight, and where was the woman he met. *"A man needs something to hold on to."* Looking at her body up and down.

This was the point where something snapped in her. Knowing he was the cause of her depression and lack of sleep triggered her. She picked up the candle on the countertop and threw it at his head. hitting him just above his eye. He shouts out "you fucking bitch" grabbing her by the neck pinning her on the bathroom wall. "I will kill you, you worthless piece of shit. Look at you. You can't even fight right." Laughing and shouting out how pathetic she looked, Lauren kicks and squirms, pushes her feet on his knees. kicking until he lets go. They both lean toward the floor. Lauren was beyond talking to. She runs out of the bathroom as he shortly follows apologizing. Baby! I am sorry. I did not mean I was going to hurt you. Heavily bleeding from the head and stumbling around the house looking for her. "Baby! Where are you!?" stupid bitch he mumbled, where are you!! He opens the laundry room to find her in the corner loading up his Glock. "What the fuck are you doing !?" snatching the gun from her. slapping her in the mouth with a hanger he pulled off the laundry rack. She screams, dropping the handful of bullets she tried to shove into the gun. Curling up in the corner where he kept hitting her with the hanger. Her screams for help echoed through the house. He finally stops hitting her, grabs her by the hair, dragging her into the bathroom, pushing her in the tub, reaches for a bottle of tile cleaner from under the cabinet, and sprays it all over her. Lauren, laying in the tub, protecting her face, crying out for help. He reached for the hanger and continued to beat her until he becomes tired. Blood dripping down his face and rage in his eyes He turned on the cold shower water and left her shaking, throwing up and whimpering. Lauren found comfort in the chilly water on her burning skin she stayed there, 25 minutes passed before he came back in to cut the water off. You dumb bitch he said, don't you ever think about pulling a gun on me. Get up! he yells. She lies still with no response. James pulled down his shorts and urinates on her. lifeless and shamed she lets out a horrible sound of pain and anger. He grabbed her out the tub onto the floor and forces himself on her. she had no fight, no energy, no expression. "Yeah, you're never going anywhere, you belong to me and will never find anyone to take care of you the way I do." Raping her, he pulls out and ejaculates on her face. As he is leaving out, he looks down at her and kicks her in the side. 'Now get the fuck up and get yourself together." In shock, Lauren gets up and showers. Her thought process was foggy. Standing in the shower with the door open, looking in the mirror, she screams, "My God help me!" "Help me please!!!" he walks in looking at her as if he were a new person, sadness, and empathy in his eye's. A personality that displayed compassion. He walked over to her, saying *"Baby, come on, let's get you to bed'* he holds out his hands for her to reach out to him. Staring in his eyes she tightly grabs hold to his arm by the elbow. In her other hand was a razor she took out a shaver, keeping eye contact with him, she squeezed onto his arm tightly and slashed his wrist several times before he had a chance to pull away. He stumbled, grabbing onto the walls and reaching for her before falling to the floor. Bleeding badly, he laid there lifeless and in shock. Lauren sat with him in silence for a while contemplating cutting her own wrist or maybe she could finish him off, but instead she decided to call 911. Placed a towel over his wrist and applied pressure.

The ambulance arrived. Taking them both to the hospital to be treated for their injuries. Lauren was admitted and treated for her physical injuries and held for an extended period after giving a statement to the hospital staff and the police. James was luck to survive. He was treated for his injuries and arrested, where he faced several criminal charges thanks to the hallway camera. He was eventually convicted of assault and domestic violence. He served 3 years in jail. Lauren got a lawyer who protected her with self-defense and later sued James for physical and emotional damages. She took time to get the help she needed. After four and a half years of support and recovery, Lauren, felt the need to reach out to James after his release. She wanted closure. Despite popular opinion, they met up in a public place.

He was very remorseful and shared his new understanding of religion. She had guilt and lots of shame confused with loving emotions that surfaced and wanted to write him a check for a couple of thousand dollars to help get him acclimated back into society. And he accepted the money. They stayed in contact from time to time. After two years, Lauren was devastated to find out James met someone at church, got married, and recently had a baby boy. Throughout their conversations, Lauren believed they were rebuilding trust and working toward forgiveness. He never once mentioned his new relationship.

Lauren opened up to us about the deep emotional and physical pain she still carries from the abuse. Despite everything, she stayed in love with James and confided that she does not believe she will ever be able to love another man the way she loved him before everything changed

✝

# Sinke

Sinke was addicted to the feeling of love, and became trapped in the illusion of it, masked by jealousy and insecurity from her husband, Kevin. To Sinke, love meant putting herself last and avoiding conflict at all costs. Her opinions and suggestions were never to challenge Kevin's. She struggled to share her accomplishments or celebrate herself because he would become irritated, even hostile in a tantrum way. Keeping the peace at home meant suffering in silence.

To her, this was a cultural norm. Her mother did it. Her grandmother did it. The women before them did the same, and they had lifelong marriages. Marriage, in Sinke's world, was a badge of honor, measured not by happiness, but by endurance. If a man saw you as worthy of being a wife and mother, you had succeeded. Her happiness didn't factor into the equation.

Kevin, too, had been raised with the same beliefs. The men in his life had women like Sinke, highly educated and successful, yet silent and obedient. Asking for more support, respect, or individuality was seen as ungrateful.

At just twenty-seven, Sinke was newly married and managing a medical staff of eighty employees. Her clinic was thriving and known for excellence. Kevin worked as a doctor at a second location, which she also managed. To outsiders, they were the perfect power couple. Their families took pride in them and often used them as examples for other young couples.

Behind closed doors, it was a different story. No one wanted to hear about their marital problems. If they ever dared to speak up, they were told to stop being selfish. It was all about status, children, and preserving tradition.

And then came the pressure to have a baby.

What no one knew was that Sinke was struggling to conceive, and Kevin blamed her every day. His jealousy only grew. Her awards, glowing reviews, and full patient roster were a constant thorn in his side. He refused to attend her award dinners or professional events. Patients began asking for her instead of him, some transferring clinics entirely.

The one person always by her side was Dr. Rown, her former assistant professor and now colleague. He attended every fundraiser, board meeting, and conference. He knew Kevin and had quietly observed the cracks in their relationship. Once, he even found her crying alone in her office. Though he never crossed a line, it was no secret in the office that he deeply admired her.

Sinke longed for support from her husband, but she never dared to question his actions. She excused his absence at events. Most nights, she came home emotionally and physically drained, only to be met with more pressure. One night, after an especially exhausting day, she tried to talk about it. Kevin cut her off, launching into his own complaints. He compared her to his mother, who "never went to bed before making sure the household was perfect."

"Those were good women," he said.

Sinke sat in silence until he fell asleep. Then she made herself tea and got ready for bed. As soon as she lay down, he pulled her close and muttered, half-asleep, "Maybe you should see your doctor. It doesn't take this long for a healthy woman to get pregnant."

She stared at the ceiling, her thoughts racing.

"Yeah," she whispered. "I'll make an appointment next week."

Walking into her clinic each morning was the highlight of her day. Her staff greeted her warmly, offering coffee and pastries from her hometown. At the triage desk, Dr. Rown was always reviewing a file, usually mentoring an intern. This morning, their eyes lingered longer than usual. A familiar chill ran down her spine. She lowered her gaze, blushing.

"Good morning, Doctor," she said.

"Doctor," he nodded back, his voice warm.

She closed the door behind her, rattled. *What was that?*

From her desk, she had a clear view of the front desk. She found herself watching him, noting every detail: how attractive he was, how he made her feel safe. Her heart raced. "What the hell is happening?" she mumbled, walking to the door, only to find Dr. Rown standing there.

"Are you okay?" he asked gently.

"Yes, I'm fine," she replied, flustered, grabbing the file from his hand. He tilted his head, unconvinced.

"You sure? You seem off. Let's sit down for a minute."

She hesitated.

"Come on, "Let's take a walk and get some real coffee, not that break room stuff. My treat."

They walked silently at first. Then, he spoke. "You know, you don't have to do everything alone. You have built something incredible here. You're a brilliant doctor. Your students admire you. But you are burning yourself out."

She sighed. "I just don't know what to do."

His face softened. "Let me help. That is why they teamed us up."

But from her expression, he realized she was not talking about work.

"Sinke," he said, gently, "are you okay? Look at me. We're a team. Talk to me."

She exhaled and began to cry.

He led her into a nearby smog-check lobby, away from prying eyes.

"I feel like I'm constantly under attack," she sobbed. "No one sees what's happening to me."

"I see you," he said. Two simple words that shattered the dam inside her.

She opened up about the pressure to get pregnant, her husband, Kevin's emotional neglect, and how lonely she felt. They talked for hours. For the first time in forever, she felt protected.

They agreed to create a sacred 10-minute check-in each morning.

That small promise changed everything.

Sinke began to feel human again. Those 10-minute meetings became the lifeline she hadn't known she needed. She looked forward to them more than anything else. She found herself staying later at work, avoiding her husband, avoiding his touch. At times, she pretended to be on her cycle just to be left alone. Which she did that night. Sleeping so peacefully she had a dream of her and Dr.

Rown, sitting at the beach looking at a baby in a stroller and he reached over to kiss her. The dream was fuzzy but felt so real. So peaceful. But she couldn't stop feeling silly for having it.

Nine months passed.

One morning, before their usual check-in, Dr. Rown walked into her office and closed the door behind him. He leaned over her desk and said:

"Leave him. I will give you the life you deserve. I have always loved you, and I always will. Tell him you want a divorce, tonight."

Sinke froze. Her eyes stretched wide, heart pounded. His words sounded impossible but ones she needed to hear. She was willing to do what was necessary for her happiness, but nervous. "I can't just…"

Then she nodded. "Okay."

As he walked out, she called after him. "What about our morning ten minutes?"

He smiled and came back. "I am about to plan an entire lifetime with the woman I adore. I will not waste another minute torturing myself. The next ten-minute meeting will be the first of our forever." Locked in on him leaving her office she was afraid, but it felt so right.

That night, Sinke arrived home to find Kevin's parents visiting again. Her heart pounded. She hesitated at the door, took a deep breath, and walked in.

"Do you always get home this late?" her mother-in-law barked." We have been waiting to have dinner. Please sit, I cooked Kevin's, favorite."

"I run a clinic," Sinke replied calmly.

"Well, you need to figure that out. What kind of wife works so much? No wonder you can't get pregnant." Sinke, looks over to her husband for a rescue instead,

Kevin just nodded. "Yeah, maybe you should listen to how Mom did it."

That was it. She knew at that moment she would always be alone and attached in their family; she could imagine them trying to turn her own children against her. Sinke, washed up for dinner and takes a set.

Traditional dishes being passed around the table with the sounds of chattering plates and silverware. Thank you for dinner Singe said to her mother-in-law. That is very kind of you. "well, my son has to have a well-cooked meal. Sinke was tired of his mother's attitude and rude comments while her husband just sat there in approval. She puts her fork down and looks at his mom and said, "I will not have you continue to come in my home disrespecting me and commenting on things that are none of your business." Now, if you have nothing kind to say you can leave." The mom became highly upset and stood up, yelling and waving her hands, telling her son to correct his wife. She turns to singe and tells her," You are a horrible wife and will be a horrible mother. The son and husband sit there quietly and allow mom to go on. 'You never invite us over and leave my son home alone. What kind of wife does that!? Sinke, Stood up and said " the kind of wife who doesn't want her husbands parents over, the kind of wife who has a more successful career, the kind of wife that has a horrible husband because he was raised by horrible parents and the kind of wife that would never bring an innocent child into a family of such horrible individuals". Leaving all three of them in shock, the husband finally speaks when his mom starts putting on an award-winning performance. Crying and screaming. "Son, oh my poor son. Come, come home with us." Sinke looks at her husband and said "no need, to go home with mommy and daddy. I will leave, and I want a divorce!" and walks upstairs for some things. The mom falls to the floor, the dad rushes over to the mom and her soon-to-be ex-husband stands there, tears flowing down his face stuck in disbelief, shock, or fear. He did not chase after her, he didn't say a word. Walking passed all of them with two suite cases and a bag she gets in her car and drove off.

Halfway down the block, she picks up her phone and books a hotel near the clinic. The next morning, she decided to work remotely. It was the right decision. She needed to decompress and find a divorce attorney. She wanted the process to be quick and was not in any condition to be at work. Dr. Rown was also on her mind, and she did not want to answer any questions or make it awkward at work. The morning was moving fast and was productive for her. She found a divorce attorney, moved her money out of their joint account, and contacted a real estate agent to sell the house. She noticed three emails from Dr. Rown, one of them subject: 10-Minute check-in. She opened it, but the body of the email was empty. She calls him on his work cell. Answering at the first ring. "Hey." Hey. she replies.

Three years later. Sinke, sat in a beachfront café, her 12-month-old son giggling in a stroller, ice cream smeared on his face. Her husband, Dr. Rown, smiling with joy reached over and placed his hand on her new baby bump and kissed her.

"Let's go home, habibi,"

✝

# The lady next door

S he judged everyone's relationships except her own. She picked people apart, critiquing them from the inside out. *"He's not good enough for her,"* she would say, or *"She's not even his type."* She lectured her friends on what they shouldn't tolerate, warning them of red flags and predicting failure. She told them to stop chasing love, to stay single, to raise their standards.

But her advice came wrapped in condescension. She mocked their choices, criticized their partners, even commented on their appearances as if love was something they didn't deserve. Their stories became her entertainment, their pain the punchline of her jokes. On the surface, she seemed composed, confident, and wise.

Yet beneath that polished exterior, her own relationship was rotting.

She was still carrying the weight of trauma from a decade-old relationship hurt she never truly healed from. Picking apart others was her coping mechanism. It was how she processed the woman she never got to become, the boundaries she never set, the life she never built.

She spoke as if she had not endured emotional and physical abuse, as if she had not faced infidelity, cruel words, and abandonment from the man she still lived with. She hid her pain behind harsh judgments, constructing a cage around her own dysfunction so that, in public, she could pretend to live a lie of freedom.

They were overly affectionate in front of others, as if trying to convince themselves they were still in love. But behind closed doors, they walked in silence, abusive silence, each waiting for the other to leave, break down, or disappear.

And so, they continued, locked in an impressive performance, bound not by love, but by a slow death neither of them dared to end.

✝

# Calvin

Calvin moved through life like someone drifting in a dream he couldn't quite wake up from. On the surface, he functioned. He held a job, showed up when it counted, cracked jokes at the right moments, but underneath it all, there was a quiet storm brewing. He wasn't truly living; he was coasting, surviving, numbing. A man with a deep and unspoken grief he had long buried, starting with the one loss he never truly processed: his mother.

Calvin did not lose his mother in the physical sense. She was still alive, still present in the world, but her presence had never been a source of comfort. Emotionally, she was absent, distant, cold, unpredictable. Calvin had been born into a space that should have felt nurturing but instead felt like walking on a tightrope. He had learned early on to scan for danger, to anticipate mood swings, to overcompensate for love that never arrived in the way he needed. In his mind, he had buried his mother long ago, not in the literal sense, but in the way a child learns to cope with abandonment. He had grieved the idea of what she should have been and accepted the reality that she never was.

This unresolved pain would shape every relationship Calvin had as an adult, especially with women. He was trapped in a cycle, drawn repeatedly to the same kind of women, the same kind of energy, the same emotional patterns. At first glance, it might have seemed like he had a "type," but it had little to do with physical appearance. It wasn't about hair color, body shape, or fashion sense. No, Calvin's "type" had everything to do with a certain emotional frequency. An edge, a fire, a certain intensity that bordered on volatility. These women often carried a chaos that mirrored his own internal state, a chaos he both resented and craved.

To Calvin, it felt like chemistry. There was a magnetic pull, a deep, aching need that stirred whenever he met someone who triggered this response in him. He mistook the adrenaline for love. The rollercoaster of highs and lows felt passionate, intoxicating, real. But what he did not understand, or didn't want to confront, was that what he labeled as "vibes" or "passion" was simply his nervous system reacting to the familiarity of dysfunction. His body was comfortable in crisis because crisis had always been home.

He knew how to operate under pressure, knew how to chase affection and survive rejection. He had been practicing it since childhood. So, when he found himself in toxic relationships, ones filled with fighting, emotional manipulation, push and pull, he would subconsciously blind out the red flags. He saw love. Or at least, his version of it.

Deep down, Calvin wasn't choosing these women intentionally to suffer. In fact, he often believed he was choosing love, something real, something intense, something that stirred his soul. What he failed to realize was that love was not supposed to hurt like that. Love wasn't supposed to feel like survival. But when survival is all, you know, love that feels safe can feel boring. Flat. Uninteresting.

Women who were stable, kind, and emotionally available often didn't make it past the first few dates. Calvin would convince himself there was "no spark" or that something was "off," when in reality, the absence of emotional chaos felt foreign, even threatening. He mistook peace for indifference and misread consistency as disinterest. His nervous system simply didn't know what to do when it wasn't being activated by drama.

So, he kept gravitating back to the women who lit emotional fires in him, the ones who mirrored the emotional instability of his early life. These relationships would start hot and fast, filled with excitement and lust, late-night conversations that seemed to dive deep into their souls. But soon enough, the cracks would show. Arguments would erupt over misunderstandings. Jealousy would seep in. Emotional games would start, and Calvin would play right along, thinking it was all part of love's twisted dance.

In reality, it was trauma bonding. It was two wounded people reenacting their pain with each other, calling it love. But Calvin didn't know any other way. He had never been shown how love was supposed to feel, safe, secure. He wasn't use to emotional safety; he was use to uncertainty, to inconsistency, to waiting for the other shoe to drop. So even when these relationships began to take a toll on him, he did not leave. He stayed. Because the pain was familiar, and familiarity felt like comfort even when it hurt.

Friends and family would sometimes try to intervene, gently pointing out the patterns. They'd ask why he stayed in relationships that drained him, why he kept chasing women who didn't seem to love him in healthy ways. Calvin would brush it off. "You wouldn't understand," he would say. "It's complicated." And it was. But not in the way he thought.

The complication wasn't in the relationships themselves; it was inside him. It was in the inner child who still yearned for a mother's love, who still thought if he could just prove himself worthy enough, loud enough, good enough, then maybe, finally, someone would stay. Someone would choose him. Someone would love him the way he had always needed to be loved.

But that little boy didn't know that healing doesn't come from reenacting the trauma until you get it right. It comes from recognizing the pattern, breaking it, and learning a new way to love, even when that new way feels foreign and uncomfortable at first.

Calvin's story isn't unique. So many people carry wounds from childhood into their adult relationships, repeating patterns without fully understanding why. But what makes Calvin's story powerful is the potential it holds, the possibility of awakening, of self-discovery, of healing. Because the moment Calvin begins to see that the chaos he is addicted to isn't love at all, it is just what he's used to and the moment everything can change.

He may still feel the pull toward chaos, but now he has a choice. He can begin the challenging work of rewiring his nervous system, of sitting with the discomfort of peace, of choosing partners who feel safe rather than thrilling. He can learn that real love might not give him the rush of adrenaline he was used to, but it will give him something far better. Stability, trust, and emotional freedom.

That process is never easy. It will require Calvin to sit with parts of himself he long avoided. To grieve the mother, he never had. To unlearn the lies he's told himself about what he deserves. To forgive himself for the choices he's made while trying to survive. But it's a journey worth taking.

Because beneath all the chaos, all the pain, and all the toxic relationships, Calvin is still that little boy, longing for love, for safety, for peace. And he deserves to find it. Not in someone else, but within himself first. Only then can he build the kind of relationships that do not drain him but nourish him. The kind that doesn't rely on drama to stay alive, but thrive on mutual respect, understanding, and care.

Calvin's past may be full of storms, but his future can be calm, not because life becomes perfect, but because he learns how to find peace in the quiet, and how to finally call peace by its name.

# Shondra

Shondra had always been drawn to the glow of other people's success, like a bee to pollen. But unlike the bee, she didn't produce anything of value She fed off of others. There was a certain artistry to the way she did it, subtle yet deliberate, calculated and cold. She never built anything of her own, not really. Instead, she had perfected the craft of attaching herself to people who had already done the groundwork. Entrepreneurs, creators, dreamers, she found them when they were just getting started, offered her help, and slowly positioned herself at the center of their stories. Later, she would rewrite the story entirely, painting herself as the mastermind behind their ascent.

To the world, she was a collaborator, a motivator, a visionary. In truth, she was a thief of ambition.

On an unusually bright Wednesday morning, Shondra walked into her favorite coffee shop on 7th and Fig. It was her sanctuary, a place where the baristas knew her name and the foam on her latte was always crafted to perfection. The smell of roasted beans mingled with fresh pastries warmed the air as she stood in line, sunglasses pushed up on her head, lips glossed and smirking.

That's when she saw him.

Tall, clean-shaven, handsome in an unassuming way. He stood directly in front of her, thumbing through a soft-cover workbook. She leaned slightly to see the title.

*"Step by Step: Building a Business Plan That Works."*

A slow smile formed. Her pulse quickened, not out of attraction, but from opportunity.

She was always observant of her surroundings. It was a skill she cultivated early in life, a sixth sense she used like a scalpel. With it, she could dissect a room, read people like pamphlets, and uncover every weakness worth exploiting. Shondra didn't just see people, she assessed them.

After ordering her drink, she stepped closer and tilted her head with practiced interest. "Good morning," she said sweetly, her voice warm like honey. "Great minds think alike. I am also working on a business plan. It's... overwhelming, isn't it?"

He looked up, surprised, then smiled politely. "Yeah, it is a lot. I'm Jeremy."

"Shondra."

He offered a hand. She shook it.

Always flirtatious, Shondra eased into conversation as naturally as if they were old friends. She spoke of ambition and burnout, of late nights and visions too big for small bank accounts. Jeremy listened, mesmerized by her beauty and her apparent drive. She pretended to be transparent, letting just enough vulnerability show to make him feel special. Before long, they were sitting together with their lattes, going over bullet points and business goals.

It wasn't long before he was completely under her spell.

They began meeting regularly, first at the café, then at his apartment. Their conversations blurred into sleepovers. The lines between professional collaboration and romance dissolved with her careful guidance. When Jeremy asked why they never went to her place, she explained with a sorrowful sigh that she was caring for her ailing grandparents. The house was full of nurses and medical equipment. It wasn't the environment for relaxation or romance.

The truth was, Shondra was in a long-term relationship with another man, someone she had met in an identical fashion, someone she had also exploited before growing bored.

Jeremy didn't question her. He believed her. She was magnetic, and he was completely drawn in.

As the weeks passed, she slowly took charge of the business venture. She offered to handle paperwork, fine-tune marketing materials, and even apply for grants. She insisted they register the business under her name in part, citing statistics about female-owned companies qualifying for funding. "It'll be easier this way," she had said, sliding forms across the table, her pen tapping lightly in encouragement.

"Trust me," she whispered once, leaning in. "We're in this together."

He nodded.

And just like she had done before, Shondra maneuvered herself into legal control. When the loan came through, along with a generous grant for women entrepreneurs, she adjusted the paperwork behind Jeremy's back, added her name to the check, and deposited the funds into a hidden account.

Then she vanished.

No calls. No texts. No emails. No traces.

At first, Jeremy was confused, concerned, even. But as the days turned to a week, then two, the truth settled in like ash. He had been conned. Deceived. Used. And the worst part was, he knew. Somewhere deep inside, his instincts had whispered that something was off. But he ignored them.

Because he wanted her to be real.

Crushed and humiliated, Jeremy did what most wouldn't. He did not go to the police. He didn't wallow. He decided to find her.

What Shondra didn't know about him is what she never bothered to ask, Jeremy was no ordinary victim. Behind the calm demeanor and soft-spoken nature was a mind built for machines. He was a coder, a data analyst, and a damn good hacker. Years of computer engineering had taught him that with just a little information, almost anything was possible.

He started with what he had: her cell number, her email, and the address of the coffee shop where they met. It wasn't much, but it was enough.

Jeremy began tracking her digital footprint. Burner accounts. VoIP numbers. Fake addresses. She had covered her tracks well, but not perfectly. It took over a month of digging, combing through public records, intercepting IP data from unsecured messages, and watching GPS pings from social media photos she didn't realize were geotagged.

Eventually, he narrowed down a three-block radius where she seemed to resurface every few days.

Why? Because she couldn't stay away from that damn latte.

Jeremy positioned himself across the street at a small sandwich shop with a clear view of the café. He sat with a coffee of his own, laptop open, camera ready. Day after day. Patient. Watching. Waiting.

Then, one Friday morning, there she was.

A sleek car pulled into the drive-thru, and there she sat, Shondra, effortlessly elegant as ever, tapping her fingers on the steering wheel. Her hair pulled into a bun, gold hoops catching the sunlight, sunglasses perched just above that same infuriating smirk.

Jeremy's heart pounded in his chest. The betrayal. The manipulation. The audacity.

He snapped several photos, documented the car's make and model, then ran the plates using connections from an old private security job. Within hours, he had her address. Within days, he had built a case. Emails, bank transfers, altered legal documents, he compiled it all.

But Jeremy wasn't just after justice. He wanted her to *know* he was coming.

He sent her a single message from an encrypted account: **"You picked the wrong one this time. I see you. Enjoy your latte."**

Shondra froze when she read it. Looking around afraid, but trying to play it cool heavy breathing, her hand shaking she dropped the phone and pulls off before getting her latte. Her confidence wavered. She was now exposed.

And for the first time, the predator knew what it felt like to be prey.

To be continued…. She is a whole story.

✝

# Rebecca

Covert narcissism was the silent storm. The wave of cowardice cloaked in charm, passive-aggressive behavior masked as humility, and an insatiable hunger for praise and validation. It's not loud like the overt type; it doesn't walk into the room and demands the spotlight. Instead, it slinks in quietly, waiting for the perfect moment to play victim, twist perceptions, and plant seeds of doubt in others. These individuals are masters of emotional manipulation, using empathy as both shield and weapon. They thrive on the sympathy of others, always subtly shifting blame and crafting stories where they appear either as the misunderstood hero or the wounded soul in desperate need of saving. Attention, no matter how they must get it, is their life force.

Rebecca had learned this the hard way.

After seven emotionally turbulent months wrapped in the arms of a man who offered only fleeting glimpses of affection and endless waves of confusion, she found herself looking eye level back at herself in a makeup mirror, half angry, half broken, but determined. She whispered the number aloud every morning: **150**. It wasn't just a number. It was a vow. One hundred and fifty days to reset, recalibrate, and rebuild. One hundred and fifty days of discipline, boundaries, and healing. A self-imposed challenge to rediscover her core, her strength, her silence, and her sanity.

It was a plan as structured as it was meaningful. Work would become her anchor. She would throw herself into projects, ignore the noise, and stop second-guessing her worth. Her body would be honored. Early workouts, clean eating, sleep, and hydration would replace the chaos of binge eating, restless nights, and anxiety-induced paralysis. Her circle would shrink, quality over quantity. Those who drained her would be gently, but firmly, removed. Even her physical environment would be overhauled. Rebecca was on a mission not just to cleanse her home, but her spirit.

She had done it before. After all, life had taught her many lessons. Pain was not new to her. What hurt more was realizing how willingly she had tolerated it. And why?

Their relationship began like a wildfire, hot, fast, and reckless. The chemistry was undeniable. She mistook intensity for intimacy and lust for love. He had a way of making her feel like the only person in the room… until he didn't. It was a cycle, passion, distance, confusion, apology, repeat. He always had just enough charm to pull her back in, just enough vulnerability to make her feel guilty for needing more, and just enough coldness to keep her chasing after the warmth.

At first, she thought she could fix it. That if she were more understanding, less emotional, more detached, he would come around. He didn't. And when she asked for more, more time, more clarity, more love, he made it clear: *"This is what it is. Take it or leave it."*

Sometimes, she could pretend that was enough. That the fragments he offered her were treasures. But other times, especially the nights when loneliness hit like a punch to the chest, she would spiral. Anger would rise, sharp and raw. War would erupt. She wasn't above yelling, crying, storming out, or slamming doors. Not because she wanted to hurt him, but because *she needed to feel heard*. The silence he used as punishment was unbearable.

Those arguments, though, always ended the same. He would pull away, retreating into the shell of a victim, framing her as the aggressor. "You're too much," he would whisper. "You need help." And somehow, she believed it.

But not anymore.

Rebecca stood taller now. Every moment of neglect, every gaslighted conversation, every tear she cried alone while he slept beside her like nothing was wrong, had led her here. To this vow. These 150 days were not about revenge. They were about resurrection.

She started by reclaiming her mornings. At 5:30 a.m., she was already moving. Yoga, journaling, herbal tea instead of caffeine-fueled anxiety. Instead of checking her phone for a text that would never come, she reached for her journal. Her pages filled with affirmations, reminders, and raw confessions. She poured it all out, so that it no longer had power over her.

Work, too, took on new meaning. She showed up with focus, dressed in intention, and spoke with a quiet confidence she hadn't felt in years. Her coworkers noticed the change, some complimented her glow, others sensed the distance. She wasn't rude, just intentional. She wasn't lonely, just selective.

She began to identify the subtle echoes of narcissism in her life, not just from him, but in other relationships too. Friends who never asked how she was. Family members who minimized her pain. Old lovers who only called when they needed a lifeline. She started pulling back. Quietly. Without announcements or drama. Just like the covert narcissists she had survived, only now, she was using the silence to protect her peace instead of provoking chaos.

Her body began to thank her, too. The daily movement, the clean food, the long walks without music, just the sound of her breathing and birds, became rituals of self-respect. She stopped dressing for attention, started dressing for joy. No more tight dresses to keep his gaze, no more lashes and heels unless *she* wanted them.

Around day 62, something shifted. She no longer felt the urge to tell him she was healing. That was progress. She didn't need him to know what he missed. She didn't care if he thought she moved on too fast or too slow. In fact, his opinion had lost its sting.

But healing isn't linear. Some days were brutal. Songs would trigger memories. A scent, a phrase, even a dream, would leave her breathless with longing or rage. On those days, she reminded herself why she started. She would revisit her journal, read the ugly truths she once denied, and cry if she needed to.

She also started therapy. For the first time, she unpacked the wounds beneath the wounds. Why had she tolerated so little? Why did she feel the need to earn love instead of expecting it freely? The answers weren't easy. Childhood, abandonment, early heartbreaks, they all played a part. But now she had words. Language gave her power. Understanding gave her freedom.

By day 100, she realized something profound: *She no longer missed him. She missed who she pretended he was.* The man she created in her mind, the potential she projected onto him, it was a fantasy. The real version? He lacked the depth to hold her complexity, the maturity to meet her halfway, or the empathy to see her pain. She loved an illusion. And now, she was learning to love reality. Even if it was lonely sometimes, it was honest.

As the 150th day approached, Rebecca didn't feel finished. She felt initiated. She had built a foundation. What came next was not about starting over but rising from solid ground. The relationship she now prioritized above all was the one with herself. Not in a cliché way, but in a radical, everyday kind of way.

She still wanted love. Of course she did. She still dreamed of connection, deep conversation, and intimacy rooted in safety. But now she knew, **she would never again settle for breadcrumbs in a famine**. No more conditional affection. No more cycles of highs and lows.

The covert narcissist would always exist in the world. But she no longer needed to engage. She could spot the signs now, the subtle guilt trips, the gaslighting, the victimhood mentality. And when she saw them, she would smile politely, turn away, and walk toward the light she had built within.

**150 days.**

It didn't just change her.

It reminded her of who she had been all along.

✝

# Shi

**Rest in peace to our dear friend, whose life was taken by her lover. We hope this brings awareness.**

Shi, was an outgoing animal lover, a bright person. Full of love and would help anyone who needed her. She was a daughter, best friend, and labor & delivery nurse. loved by many. New moms would come back to the hospital to thank her for the care they received, just beautiful inside and out. Shi and I met at work, both LD nurses dedicated to our careers, and instantly became besties. My wife also worked at the hospital but in the psychiatric department. I introduced them at lunch one day, and she also felt the same. I mean, her personality was life. after a few months, we all went on a double date and was introduced to her girlfriend. Almost immediately, my wife and I saw that they were not only the complete opposite, but the girlfriend was extremely controlling and triggered by Shi's bubbly personality. At the concert, she didn't seem to be enjoying herself and walked off quite a few times. Dinner was uncomfortable because she barely talked, and Shi made multiple excuses for her behavior. That night, we saw a different person in our friend and my wife, with twenty-five years as a psychiatrist, picked up things I didn't. We continued with our night and tried not to judge. Everyone has an off day or two and it is not our business, right? It's what most people would think and do as we did.

Four years of being blessed with her light, our hearts were shredded into pieces when we got the news that our beloved friend was savagely stabbed to death multiple times by her girlfriend in a jealous rage one night. It was reported by neighbors that the GF asked Shi, about a text message that came in at 11:30 pm from one of her private clients she was supporting as her birthing Doula. There was one-sided shouting and things being thrown in their condo. Shortly after calling the police, they heard several horrible screams and silence. The GF allegedly stripped out her bloody clothes and took a swim in the pool, where she waited for the police to arrive.

Shi lived a life in painful silence. She was an amazing person who never spoke badly of her relationship. We all can't help but feel guilty for not getting involved, at least asking how the relationship was going and bringing light to the flashing warning signals we saw. It was concerning behavior laced with control, manipulation, and jealousy, but never could we imagine this.

In memory of our dear friend Shi, R.

# Interesting Information

## 1. Erosion of Self-Esteem and Identity

One of the most profound impacts of a narcissistic relationship is the gradual erosion of the victim's self-esteem. Narcissists often engage in a pattern of devaluation, where they initially idealize their partner and then slowly begin to criticize, belittle, and undermine them. This cycle of idealization and devaluation can be confusing and emotionally destabilizing.

Victims may begin to internalize the narcissist's negative messages, believing they are unworthy, unlovable, or inadequate. This can lead to a loss of self-confidence and, in some cases, a complete breakdown of personal identity. Over time, the partner may become a shell of their former self, questioning their worth and losing sight of their goals, values, and desires.

## 2. Emotional Manipulation and Gaslighting

Narcissists are often highly skilled at manipulation. One common tactic is **gaslighting**, where the narcissist distorts facts or denies events in order to make the victim doubt their reality. For example, if a partner confronts a narcissist about a hurtful comment, the narcissist might respond with, "You're too sensitive," or "That never happened." Over time, victims may begin to question their memory, perception, and sanity.

This emotional manipulation keeps the victim off-balance and more easily controlled. The narcissist maintains power by confusing their partner and making them feel dependent. The longer this dynamic continues, the more the victim becomes isolated, unsure of their own emotions and experiences.

## 3. Chronic Anxiety and Depression

Living in a constant state of emotional uncertainty can take a significant toll on mental health. Many people in narcissistic relationships experience chronic anxiety, always walking on eggshells to avoid triggering their partner's rage or disapproval. This environment of psychological stress can lead to panic attacks, insomnia, and other anxiety-related disorders.

Depression is another common consequence. Victims often feel trapped, hopeless, and emotionally drained. They may experience a sense of mourning for the relationship they thought they had, or the person the narcissist pretended to be at the beginning. The loss of control, isolation, and emotional abuse can combine to create deep, enduring depression that sometimes requires professional intervention.

## 4. Isolation and Social Withdrawal

Narcissists often look to control their partners not only emotionally but also socially. They may work to isolate their partner from friends, family, or anyone who might offer a supportive perspective. This could be done overtly, by forbidding contact with certain people, or more subtly, by constantly creating drama or tension that makes social interactions difficult.

As the victim becomes more isolated, the narcissist's power increases. Without external validation or perspective, the partner becomes more susceptible to the narcissist's influence. This isolation also makes it more difficult for victims to leave the relationship, as they feel they have nowhere to turn.

## 5. Loss of Trust in Future Relationships

After escaping a narcissistic relationship, many individuals struggle with trust. Having been manipulated and deceived, it becomes difficult to believe that others have good intentions. Victims may carry emotional baggage into new relationships, fearing a repeat of the same dynamic.

This loss of trust can lead to hyper-vigilance, commitment issues, and difficulty forming deep emotional connections. Rebuilding a sense of safety and intimacy takes time and often requires therapy or self-reflection. The effects of the trauma do not end when the relationship ends, they often echo for years afterward.

## 6. Codependency and Trauma Bonding

Many victims of narcissistic abuse develop codependent behaviors. This happens when their self-worth becomes entirely tied to the narcissist's approval. Victims may begin to neglect their own needs and prioritize the narcissist's happiness in hopes of regaining their affection or avoiding conflict. In some cases, a phenomenon known as **trauma bonding** occurs. This is a psychological response where the victim develops a deep emotional attachment to the abuser due to intermittent reinforcement, cycles of abuse followed by affection or apologies. These bonds can be incredibly difficult to break, as the victim becomes emotionally addicted to the highs and lows of the relationship.

## 7. Physical Symptoms and Somatic Effects

Emotional abuse does not only manifest psychologically, but it can also have physical consequences. Victims may experience headaches, gastrointestinal issues, fatigue, or chronic pain due to prolonged stress and anxiety. These somatic symptoms are the body's response to being in a constant state of fight or flight.

Some individuals may also develop eating disorders, substance abuse problems, or self-harming behaviors as a way to cope with the emotional pain. It's important to recognize that the physical health of a person in a narcissistic relationship is often just as affected as their mental health.

## 8. Post-Traumatic Growth and Recovery

Despite the damage, it is possible to heal after a narcissistic relationship. Many survivors eventually experience **post-traumatic growth**, a phenomenon where individuals come out stronger, wiser, and more self-aware after enduring psychological trauma. Healing often involves therapy, education on narcissistic abuse, rebuilding social support networks, and reclaiming a lost sense of identity. The recovery process may be long and nonlinear, but with time and support, survivors can rediscover their inner strength and learn to set healthier boundaries in future relationships. Many go on to become advocates for others in similar situations, using their experience to help others break free from abuse.

Being in a narcissistic relationship can have devastating effects on one's mental, emotional, and even physical well-being. The manipulation, gaslighting, and emotional abuse can strip a person of their confidence, isolate them from their support system, and leave long-lasting psychological scars. However, with awareness, support, and therapeutic guidance, healing is not only possible, but it can also lead to profound personal growth. Survivors can learn to recognize red flags, reclaim their sense of self, and build healthier, more fulfilling relationships in the future.

# Erica & Gregory

She met Gregory, an American man working temporarily in her country, and the connection was instant. They quickly became inseparable, spending countless hours together, both in person and on long, late-night phone calls. She showed him around Europe, while he swept her off her feet with promises of a grand future. He claimed to be a successful businessman back in the States, with money, property, and everything a man could want, except a wife.

What captivated her most wasn't just the charm or the promises, but his deep knowledge of the Bible. A self-proclaimed Christian, he could recite scripture from memory, breaking down verses in ways that stirred something in her. Raised as an atheist, she found his spiritual wisdom compelling, even necessary. For the first time, she saw a unique way to live, one that felt purposeful, even holy.

Two and a half years later, Gregory's overseas assignment ended. Despite her family's concerns, Erica packed up her life and moved to America, pregnant with their first child and full of hope for the lavish lifestyle he had painted so vividly.

The journey was exhausting. She battled nausea throughout the flight and found the cramped coach seat difficult to endure. "Doesn't your company offer business or first-class for international travel?" she asked him. He brushed it off, quoting scripture and gently reminding her not to be ungrateful.

She let it go. After all, she loved him, his charm, their intimacy, and now the life growing inside her. Still, by the time they landed, her patience was wearing thin. Seated near the back of the plane, she fought the urge to rush forward and just escape the cramped cabin. But she held back, knowing any complaint might spark tension.

Outside the airport, he picked up a rental car and drove her to what he called "home." They pulled up to a sleek, modern condominium near the waterfront, surrounded by quaint boutiques, cozy coffee shops, and trendy restaurants. For a moment, she felt at ease. The location was beautiful, inviting.

But as they stepped inside, she noticed how bare it was. The condo was clean, impeccably so, but it lacked warmth. It felt more like a place for a man passing through than a home meant for building a family. And though she said nothing, a quiet unease began to settle in. Erica wanted to believe everything he had told her. The views were beautiful, the neighborhood peaceful and upscale, but something didn't feel right. The house lacked any sign of permanence: no pictures, no paperwork, no storage, no personal touches. Still, they continued settling in.

It was time to start buying things for the baby and setting up a nursery. But when Erica mentioned going shopping and suggested converting the office space into a bedroom, everything changed. He became furious, yelling, calling her ungrateful, and reciting scripture again.

He told her she would never make it to the Kingdom of God because of her selfish and greedy nature. He accused her of being materialistic, claiming she only cared about herself and would be a terrible mother because of it.

Erica was crushed. She immediately felt the need to defend herself, to explain that she just wanted to make their house a home. But he snapped back coldly:

"This is not your home. You came here with nothing but the clothes on your back. Good luck going back home, your family will only see you as a failure. And you are not taking my baby with you. We can't afford to stay here now because you got pregnant on purpose. You only think about yourself. And now we have to move."

She sat there in silence, tears streaming down her face. Afraid to respond, afraid to escalate his anger any further, she was left stunned, heartbroken, confused by his words, and shaken by the sudden shift in his behavior.

Two weeks before the baby was due, they had to move. That's when she discovered the place they were living in was actually a short-term rental, managed under his cousin's LLC. She also found out his "job" was just a series of temporary assignments, side gigs that allowed him to travel occasionally, but offered no real stability.

She didn't have the time or energy to be angry, to confront him, or to ask the tough questions. They were a family now, and she had to go into damage control mode. She found herself constantly lying to her own family, backing up his claims that life in the States was everything he had promised, stable, secure, and even better than expected.

In reality, they had moved into a far less desirable place, and soon after, the baby was born. Pressure from her family started mounting. They were full of questions: Why weren't they married yet? When could they visit? They had seen the photos on social media of a waterfront condo and assumed that was where she was living.

They were eager to meet the baby and spend time with the new family in the U.S. But the anxiety of keeping up the illusion was eating away at her. Her explanations were starting to sound less believable, even to herself, and certainly to others.

After just five months at their new place, they were hit with an eviction notice. Thirteen years into this cycle, it had become normal for their son to leave behind schools and friends. They were constantly moving, bouncing from one place to the next. Gregory had resorted to using fake identities to secure new rentals.

Erica wasn't allowed to work, yet she was expected to support his ventures by scouting out new opportunities. She did what she could, supporting him in any way possible while trying to hold together a life that was falling apart. As their son grew older, he began to speak up for his mother during arguments, asking his father direct questions. But Gregory twisted his son's empathy, using it to further undermine Erica. He poisoned their son's reality of her, always using scripture to manipulate the story.

The truth was, Gregory was a hypocrite. He didn't live by the teachings he preached. He cherry-picked Bible verses to suit his agenda and ignored everything else. Erica had converted to Christianity because of him, but he only allowed her to study the Bible under his supervision.

After years of living in emotional turmoil, Erica finally reached out to a woman they had met at a church event, someone Gregory had introduced her to. Unlike him, this woman was kind, discerning, and had always sensed something was off about their relationship. On a few occasions, she even worried that there might be physical abuse involved.

Through this new friendship, Erica began asking questions about the Bible and its true meanings. She longed to understand it better, not just to defend herself, but in the hope that knowing the Word more deeply might help Gregory see the error in his ways. She wasn't confident yet, but she was trying. She wanted to stand on her own faith, not the version of it that had been used to control her.

The woman from church had made a heartfelt commitment to be there for Erica. Over time, the two became very close, like family. Feeling that this friend was a safe and trustworthy presence, especially because of their shared faith, Erica began confiding in her about her home life. Eventually, she even invited her friend over, believing it was a safe space to do so.

But it didn't take long for the friend to notice that something was concerning.

Though Gregory also knew her from church, he acted oddly whenever she visited. If Erica were enjoying herself or simply laughing, Gregory would suddenly call her into another room and remain there, disrupting the moment. Erica would return looking embarrassed, drained, and fatigued. It became clear that her husband's behavior made visitors deeply uncomfortable, many would quietly stop coming around. But her church friend stayed. She remained loyal to their friendship and tried to support Erica however she could, especially when Gregory was not around, whether by visiting or calling to check in.

One night, Erica called her in tears. She said Gregory had pushed her into a wall, in front of their son, and that they were being evicted. That night, Erica began to open up more. She told her about Gregory's long history of online relationships with women overseas. He had been sending them money, iPhones, and other gifts, all while lying to them about his "crazy" wife he claimed he was planning to leave. He had even been planning to travel and meet these women, marketing himself as available and ready for a new life. one of the women was noticeably young looking, like 15, and was sending nudes he asked for. It was sickening.

Erica had found and printed out emails to confront him, and that is when he pushed her. She was devastated, not just by the betrayal, but by the realization that she had sacrificed so much for a man who had no intention of protecting or prioritizing his family. She had left her own family, stood by him, and believed in a future that was never real.

Her emotions long suppressed, were now boiling over, and her friend feared she might do something drastic. The tension escalated so severely that a neighbor ended up calling the police. Erica was found in the hallway, screaming, releasing all the pain she had held in for so long. Adding to it, it was the same week, they were forced to leave their home.

That night, before the police arrived, he left the scene.

And his solution?

Instead of facing the damage he caused, he went right back to searching for a wife online, sending money and gifts to strangers, scammers while his own family struggled to survive. He never returned to the apartment. He left her to pack up their lives alone.

With no job, no money, and completely at the mercy of others, Erica did what she could. She and her son pulled out what few belongings they could salvage before the sheriff arrived. That night, they slept in the car, parked on the curb, watching what remained of their lives until help could come in the morning.

Erica felt deflated. Lost. The car they slept in was already being tracked by the bank for repossession. She removed the license plates and nervously dozed off with one eye open, fear pressing on her chest.

Her son, crying softly in the back seat, reached out for her hand. She gripped it tightly.

"I'll never leave you," she whispered.

"Promise," he said. Erica held back her tears and said, 'I promise, sweetheart, it's us forever.'

In that moment, they both understood, they were all the other had.

# Amelia, Donte & Tasha

Amelia's longing for Donte was like a moth drawn to a flame. beautiful, reckless, and ultimately destructive.

What began as a childhood crush evolved into decades of tangled emotion: seduction, regret, and a bond that felt otherworldly. It was as if they had been lovers across lifetimes. Their connection was magnetic, intoxicating, both natural and entirely forbidden.

Donte was married. He was her addiction, her comfort, her poison, and her antidote.

For years, they found solace in each other's arms, while his wife, Tasha, endured in silence, choosing to keep their family intact rather than tear it apart.

It was a love triangle lived out one household at a time.

A secret pregnancy. A lonely abortion. A heartbreak Amelia carried alone.

They reconnected at a public event, as if the universe had answered an unspoken call-one neither of them had dialed, yet both had desperately needed. It was a quiet intervention, drawing them together to save each other from falling into something far more destructive.

Amelia, recently divorced from a charming con artist, was left shaken and guarded. She was afraid to explore her desires in unfamiliar spaces, overwhelmed by shame, unhealed wounds, and a lingering sense of embarrassment. Emotionally abandoned and financially exploited, she was stuck in survival mode-navigating life with walls around her heart and a deep need she didn't yet know how to name.

Donte, newly married and the father of a baby girl, found himself slowly unraveling beneath the weight of a life he no longer recognized. His wife, buried beneath the heavy fog of postpartum depression, had grown distant-physically present but emotionally unreachable. The home they built together felt colder by the day, and Donte, once a source of strength, now felt invisible.

The quiet ache of neglect crept in slowly, unforgiving, and sharp. His needs-emotional, physical, spiritual-went unheard, and when he tried to speak them aloud, he was met with silence or shame. He stopped asking. Stopped hoping. But the ache didn't leave. Instead, it pushed him to the edge. He was exhausted, stripped down to survival instincts, and desperate for a glimpse of warmth-any sign that he was still alive beneath it all. He would have risked anything for a moment of peace. For a touch that did not feel burden. For a sliver of happiness that didn't come with guilt. Both good people bouncing around like faces in a nostalgic Pac-Man game.

As their eyes met, it felt like the end of a long, silent search, an overwhelming relief, as if they had finally found what they had been missing. They embraced, grinning uncontrollably, oblivious to the world around them. Who was watching, who might judge- it didn't matter. In that moment, they were wrapped in something pure, something that felt like heaven. It wasn't just an embrace- it was home.

To outsiders, it may have looked like chaos, even confinement. But to them, it was the start of something deeply peaceful, something real. Their situation-misunderstood by many-was about to unfold into something uniquely theirs. Despite what the world might label as infidelity, this was their truth. A love story not just for this life, but one meant to echo into the next.

To those unfamiliar with their story, it may seem foolish-something to scoff at or judge from a distance. And even those who do know it might still carry the same jealousy, the same critical gaze. But if you look closer, if you remember deeper, you might recognize them not just as lovers in this life, but as souls bound across time. You might know them as a version of Ramesses the Great and Queen Nefertiti, despite current circumstances, it is just two hearts destined to find each other, again and again.

The first time they were alone, they spent hours talking at her place about old times and mutual friends. As she walked him to the door, he gently touched the right side of her face and leaned in, delivering one of the most passionate kisses she had ever experienced. Her body weakened, and the intensity of their connection surged through every fiber of her being, reaching deep into her bones.

She pulled back, her gaze filled with confusion, wondering how he had ignited a fire within her, a fire she had always longed to see reflected in another. It wasn't something she had ever read about or witnessed; it was something wild and alive inside her, something she had only dreamed of setting free. As she turned to walk away, her eyes lingered, silently inviting him to stay.

Backing into her bedroom, she stood there speechless, almost in a trans, giving him strong signals, submitting her body to his mind, his movement and story. She could read him from every touch. His worries, his sadness. Hesitation flooded in her like a river. Even the sound of his voice moved her. Who are you? she wondered, locking in closer. Once he went inside of her, she felt in sync, she was in total submission, the way he sucked her breast, moan and held on to her tightly. Every intimate connection from that point on would be like poetry. *"In the hush between two hearts, where words grow soft and eyes speak loud, there lives a peace, deep as oceans, a warmth not lit by fire, but by the quiet knowing: I am seen, and I am home."* Overcome with a sense of DeJ a'Vu, instantly, she knew they would always be together.

Months had passed, and they spent every possible moment together talking and texting two, sometimes three times a day, from sunrise to sunset. The intensity between them grew, fueled by desire and an undeniable passion. She craved him deeply. Her mind was open, her heart at ease, willing to spend her life in his shadow.

The love they shared was essential, like air, bringing them alive, whole, and inseparable. When apart, they felt physically ill, as though something vital was missing. They had become utterly addicted to one another.

By the fourth-month mark, Amelia found out she was pregnant. Fear gripped her at the thought of telling Donte. Their arrangement was already unconventional, and the idea of adding more pressure terrified her. What if this was the thing that pushed him away? What if he turned his back on her, and their unborn child? The possibility of raising a baby alone, abandoned, and heartbroken, haunted her. How would she ever explain that to her child?

Worse yet, what if Donte *wanted* the child and told his wife about their relationship? That revelation could spark a new wave of chaos. Amelia already suspected his wife had her own suspicions and could use that knowledge to force him to stay away entirely. The idea of their child growing up in the shadows, in conflict and rejection, felt cruel. What would Donte's family think? How much pain would a child absorb from the choices adults had made?

These thoughts overwhelmed her. She didn't want to bring a child into a life of bitterness, secrecy, and regret. She didn't want Donte to grow to resent her, or worse, the child. And yet, deep down Amelia also knew that the baby, conceived in a moment of true connection, could be the ultimate expression of their love. A perfect blend of the two of them. A symbol of something real in the middle of so much confusion.

At eight weeks, the decision couldn't wait much longer. Time was pressing in from all sides.

She kept seeing Donte, aching to tell him, but the words never seemed to come. Inside, she was falling apart. The thought of going through a procedure she didn't truly believe in, not only physically risky, but morally complicated for her, was tearing her apart. She had always judged others for making that choice. Now, she was facing it herself, and her heart was in shambles.

One rainy night, Donte called and told her he was coming over. She felt it in her gut: *"This is the night. I must tell him"*

When he arrived, the rain was coming down in sheets, thunder rumbling through the sky like a warning. It felt like the world outside mirrored everything inside her, chaotic, turbulent, sad.

He walked in and pulled her into a hug. She clung to him tightly, trying to hide her puffy eyes and racing heart. She didn't want to let go, and for a long moment, he didn't either. He melted into the embrace, the kind that spoke more than words ever could. But then he gently pulled back and led her by the hand to sit on the couch.

"I need to tell you something," Amelia began, her voice soft and shaking.

But before she could go on, his phone buzzed. Then again. And again.

Donte glanced at the screen and his expression turned apologetic, even guilty. "I'm so sorry, I have to take this. Just two minutes, I promise," he said, kissing her cheek before disappearing into the other room.

It was Tasha, his wife. She never called while he was with Amelia. Never sent multiple texts. But that night was different. That night, it was like she sensed a shift in the battlefield. Like she knew she had to cross enemy lines.

Amelia sat there in silence, her chest tight, her stomach churning. She listened to his muffled voice, trying to remain composed as her emotions surged with the hormones of early pregnancy. Tears pricked her eyes, but she held them in.

She heard him ask softly, "What would you like me to do?"

Tasha's voice came through faintly, sharp and commanding: "Come home."

And he said, "Okay."

The silence that followed was deafening.

Donte walked back into the living room with a heavy expression. "I am so, so sorry. The power's out at the house. She is scared. I have to go."

Thunder cracked loud enough to shake the windows as he pulled her into another hug.

"I am so sorry," he whispered again. "I'll call you when I'm in the car."

Amelia stood frozen, unable to move, barely able to speak. Reality had just hit her like a carefully aimed arrow. She looked down, her voice barely a whisper. "Okay… okay."

He rushed toward the door, pausing for one last glance back. "Please lock the door," he said.

And then he was gone.

She stayed in that same spot for what felt like forever, knowing deep down what her decision would be. This, *this* was what she would be dealing with. This kind of goodbye, this level of uncertainty, this imbalance. If she had the child, they would always come second. Always be a secret. Or they would live a chaotic and vengeful existence if he decided to tell her. Either way they would live in the shadows of someone else's life.

She walked into her bedroom and collapsed onto the bed, curling up into herself. Then came the sobs, loud, uncontrollable, primal. She cried until she vomited, running back and forth to the bathroom between waves of heartbreak and nausea.

Donte called repeatedly. The phone vibrated endlessly across the nightstand. Eventually, she picked it up and threw it across the room.

She cried herself to sleep that night, the storm outside finally beginning to quiet, but inside, the storm raged on.

The next morning, she slept in late. It was noon. It felt as if an angel had watched over her through the night, she had not slept that soundly in weeks. The room was calm, bathed in soft gold light as the sun peeked through the curtains.

She stretched, the silence hugging her gently. Sliding out of bed, she walked over to the patio and opened the door. The air was crisp and damp, still carrying the scent of last night's storm. She stepped outside barefoot, letting the cool floor ground her. The sky was wide and blue; the kind of blue that only comes after everything has been washed clean. Tilting her head back, she closed her eyes and inhaled deeply, as if trying to absorb peace itself.

Then she saw it.

To her right, arcing quietly across the sky like a whispered promise, was a rainbow, vibrant, unapologetic, and undeniable. She stood there for almost thirty minutes, just breathing and watching. Letting herself be still.

Eventually, reality tapped her on the shoulder. Today was the day. She had to make that call, the one she had been avoiding. The one that would begin the process of something she was not ready for. One of the hardest things in her life.

With a quiet sigh, she walked back inside, moving through the stillness of her apartment. She reached for her phone, and her heart stuttered. Several missed calls. A handful of texts. All from Donte.

She unlocked the screen.

*"Hey, just checking on you."*

*"You, okay?"*

*"I know last night was heavy. Call me if you want."*

*"I'll be around all day, just thinking about you."*

*"Please call me."*

His words were warm, careful. Not pushy, but present. She could feel it in the way he wrote, he knew. He felt the shift in her, even through the silence. And he hadn't disappeared.

She sat on the edge of her bed, the phone in her lap, staring at his name on the screen.

Should she call him back now?

Or should she call the doctor first?

She decided to call the doctor. She knew she would fall apart if she called Donte instead, this was not something you could talk about over the phone. She had made up her mind to stand on her own and do what was best for her situation.

Shaking with fear, she contacted her provider and scheduled a consultation for a pregnancy termination.

In the days leading up to the appointment, she saw Donte several times. She tried to avoid him but could not. As much as she wanted distance, she needed him even more. She longed to connect with him on every level, searching for something, anything, to anchor her, to pull her from the weight of her thoughts. She needed him.

A week later, the appointment arrived. She completed her consultation and was given a date for the procedure, reminded that time was critical, she was already nearing ten weeks.

That night, she met up with Donte as usual. She clung to him, more affectionate than ever, and quietly cried in his arms. They lay together in silence.

Quiet tears ran down her hidden face, her body finally at peace. His presence always brought calm, effortless, natural. He was made for her. And though it hurt to share him, life without him was unbearable.

They slept until six a.m.

She woke to find him watching her, his eyes tracing the outline of her body. He always woke up before her and watched her sleep but, this time a flicker of paranoia stirred, had he noticed a change in her?

He smiled softly.

"Good morning. You are so beautiful," he whispered, kissing her gently.

"I have to go, I'll see you later."

Every time he left, he took a small piece of her heart with him. But knowing he would return, that hope was the fragile glue that kept her whole.

She sat up and hugged him, swallowing the words she longed to say: *I love you.*

Instead, she smiled, letting him go. The next two days were nerve-wrecking for her. The next two days were agonizing. Her procedure was scheduled for Friday at 7 a.m., giving her the weekend to recover before returning to work on Monday. But the looming weight wasn't just the procedure, it was the pressure of pretending everything was normal. Since reconnecting, they had spent every weekend together. How could she explain her absence?

It had to be done.

*What do I do?* she thought. *How can I keep him away without making him suspicious?*

She knew she had to be strategic, keep her emotions buried deep. So, she called a close friend and confided in her. The friend agreed to help but took the opportunity to bring up her past abortion, reminding Amelia of how strongly she had once opposed it and now that it was her turn she would feel what she was feeling. The judgment stung. It was more than Amelia could handle.

In that moment, she changed her mind.

"Yeah… I will call you if I need you," she said instead.

Friday arrived faster than she had expected. Amelia drove herself to the clinic, keeping her head low and hoodie up as she rushed inside. She stood in a hospital gown, answering a nurse's questions:

"Is anyone forcing you to do this?"

"Do you have a ride home?"

"Are you okay to continue?"

Amelia nodded yes to all three, though her heart told a different story. She was led into a dim room and took a deep breath. As she lay down, her heart pounded. She blinked at the sterile light above her.

"Amelia," the nurse said gently. "I'm here. You are going to be okay. Hold my hand."

The anesthesiologist administered the medication. Tears streamed down Amelia's cheeks as visions of protestors' signs flashed through her mind. In a split second, she wanted to get up and say *never mind.* But the monitor betrayed her distress.

"Start counting backwards from ten," the nurse said.

She remembered reaching three before everything faded to black.

Thirty minutes later, she was being gently shaken awake by a different nurse.

"Amelia… Amelia, I need you to sit up, hun."

Around her was other women all packed in the room. Beds close to each other, rail to rail as they slowly stirred from their procedures. Amelia tried to open her eyes but quickly shut them again. The tears returned, this time louder, harder. Her body trembled as she cried out.

One woman's voice broke through, dry and detached:

"What's she crying for?"

Another responded softly, "Because it's hard. Some of us want to have a child, but… it's not ideal. This is the choice she made."

Amelia cried even harder. That same woman in the bed next to her wrapped her in an embrace, whispering, "It's okay," as her own tears fell. For a moment, Amelia felt comfort, surrounded by quiet faces who knew exactly what this moment meant.

The nurse left them to reset.

With the help of a stranger, Amelia pulled herself together just enough to take her medication and drink fluids. She completed the discharge process, got her prescription, and waited in the dressing room while a nurse went to find her ride.

Except… she did not have one.

"Who's picking you up again?" the nurse asked.

She hesitated.

"Donte," was the first name to come to mind. she lied. "He's in the car."

"Call him to come in. I can't let you leave alone."

Amelia stared at her phone. She wanted to call him, desperately. She needed him in that moment, no questions asked. But she couldn't bear the shame. She could not face her friend either.

Then she noticed clinic staff leaving through a side door.

Amelia took her chance. She slipped out behind them, made it to the parking lot, crawled into the back seat of her car, and passed out for an hour.

When she woke, she drank what was left of her water, gathered her strength, and drove herself home. On the way, she stopped at the pharmacy. Sitting in the car for what felt like forever, she finally forced herself out, hunched over, sore, and drained. A man passing by asked, "Are you okay?"

She nodded, holding her stomach, barely making it back to her car.

At her apartment, she discovered the elevator was broken. Of course it was. Everything felt like punishment. She climbed the stairs to her second-floor apartment, step by painful step, unlocked the door, took her meds, and cried herself to sleep.

She slept for hours.

When she finally woke up, her phone was buzzing with missed calls and messages, mostly from Donte. One stood out:

**"This isn't like you. Are you okay? I came to your place and no answer."**

Staring at her phone, she realized none of it felt like her. But she convinced herself she had to be okay with not feeling like herself anymore. So, she buried it, deep hoping it would never rise to the surface again.

She spent the rest of the day in silence, battling to hide the pain while her body tried to heal. The next morning, she returned missed calls with a simple excuse: she wasn't feeling well and had just started her period. It was a lie she had to make him believe, for now. She would figure the rest out later.

In the middle of her explanation, he interrupted.

"Open the door," he said.

"What?" she asked, startled.

"Amelia, I am at your door. Open up."

She moved slowly, shoving the medicine and clinic paperwork into a drawer before making her way to the door. When she opened it, he stood there, his eyes full of suspicion and distrust. She could not hold his gaze. Instead, she leaned her head against his chest, whispering, "I'm just not feeling well," while holding back tears. "Come lie down with me."

Sensing something was off, he took off his shoes and lay next to her. He did most of the talking, telling her how worried he had been, how not hearing from her made him imagine the worst. He asked her to be more mindful of how that affected him. She nodded quietly and curled into him like he was one giant pillow.

For a month, the weight of it lingered. She came up with excuse after excuse, an irregular cycle, a yeast infection, anything to avoid being intimate in that way. She found other ways to satisfy him, waiting until she was finally out of the woods.

Time passed, and they returned to their version of "normal." But something in her had changed. She had become more guarded, more sensitive settled in their dysfunctional love. She felt like a new woman, one carrying quiet pain, deep regret, fresh fears, and the ache of self-abandonment.

Morally conflicted, she grew into her choices and stood silently in the ruins of her emotions loving him from the shadows and never letting go.

†

# The Illusion of Sweetness.

When her enough had enough, it was all bad for him.

He was the kind of man who thrived on control not the obvious, stomping, shouting kind of control. No, his dominance wore a smile, cloaked in affection, disguised as care. At first, it was almost flattering. He would say things like, *"I love how red nail polish looks on you, it matches my shirt. You should wear it when we go out."* It was sweet, in a way. Romantic, even.

Then came the subtle nudges: *"Babe, do you really need to eat again? You just had lunch two hours ago."* Or *"Carbs make you sluggish, you know. Try this protein shake instead."* And before she could track the pattern, her days were scheduled around his preferences, his workouts, his meals, his moods. Her favorite coffee? Gone. Her lazy Sunday brunches? A distant memory. Her phone buzzed less. Friends stopped calling. Invitations faded.

It wasn't that she meant to push people away. But explaining *him* was hard. He was charming. Too charming. To her friends, he was the perfect boyfriend: always posting cute photos, surprising her with gifts, planning elaborate date nights. But those gifts came with expectations. That attention came with surveillance. The date nights were more about how they looked to others than how they felt to her.

Her family noticed first.

"Why haven't you visited in months?" her mother asked during a rare phone call.

"I've just been busy… you know, with him," she would say, brushing it off. But even her voice sounded distant to herself.

What she didn't say was that he hated when she visited home. "They don't really understand you like I do," he would whisper, planting seeds of doubt. "They think they know you better. But we are building our own life."

At some point, *her life* had quietly become *his plan.*

The final straw wasn't dramatic. No screaming match, no public outburst. It came on a Thursday afternoon. He had called her three times back-to-back because she had not responded in five minutes. She was in a meeting. When she finally answered, breathless and apologetic, he said coldly, "You're always ignoring me. What else do you have to do that is more important than me?"

She stared at her reflection in the bathroom mirror at work, her phone trembling in her hand.

She didn't recognize herself.

Tired eyes. Hair pulled back hastily. Her clothes felt like armor, too tight, too perfect. Every decision that day from her nail polish to the salad she forced down at lunch, had been pre-approved by him.

That is when it hit her.

She was living someone else's life.

She didn't leave that day. But something inside her cracked open.

She started small. Wore pink nail polish the next week a color he once called "childish." When he raised his eyebrow, she simply smiled and said, "I like it."

She bought herself a caramel latte and didn't log it in the calorie-tracking app he made her use.

She called her sister and stayed on the phone for two hours. She laughed. Real, belly-deep laughter, the kind she hadn't heard in months.

She reconnected with a college friend for lunch. Wore a sundress he didn't like. Ate fries and did not explain herself.

Each tiny act felt like defiance. But it also felt like her.

Eventually, he noticed.

"You've been distant," he said one night, arms crossed.

"No," she replied calmly, "I've just been myself."

He didn't like that answer.

The argument that followed was long, ugly, and filled with guilt-tripping. He listed everything he had done for her. Called her ungrateful. Questioned her loyalty. Accused her of changing.

"I have changed," she said quietly. "I'm remembering who I was before you decided who I should be."

She left a week later.

It was not easy. He cried, begged, and apologized. Promised therapy, promised change. Promised to "let her be herself."

But she had heard that tune before. Many, many times before and she was not dancing to his rhythm anymore.

Her first night alone felt like standing in the middle of a storm. Loud. But beautiful. Freeing.

She cried.

Not because she missed him. But because she finally missed herself, she was coming back.

Rebuilding wasn't easy. Some days she still checked her phone too often. Still felt the phantom weight of his disapproval. Still wondered if she was being "too much."

But more and more, she took up space.

She joined a book club. Danced at a friend's wedding. Took a solo weekend trip. Sat at a café without pretending to like almond milk.

Slowly, life stopped being a performance.

She learned to trust her choices. To forgive herself for staying so long. To cherish the strength, it took to leave.

People often think that breaking free from someone toxic happens in one bold, dramatic moment.

But for her, it was a series of quiet rebellions. Of remembering what joy tasted like. Of realizing she never needed permission to be herself.

When her enough had enough, it wasn't just bad for him, it was the end of his reign over her life.

But for her?

It was the beginning.

✝

*"Don't pray for vision and squint when the truth is revealed."*

+

# Cherish

**I'm choosing to stay focused on my healing journey and share my story from a place of growth and self-love.**

I'm proud of myself, not just for finding the strength to leave, but for loving myself enough to not go back that final time. That was the hardest part. By the time his mask finally slipped, I was already knee-deep in his cycle of toxicity.

I didn't notice how much the world around me and within me had changed. I didn't pause long enough to recognize what was happening to my mind, body, and spirit. The weight crept on, pound by pound. My skin became hypersensitive. My hair lost its shine. My energy was depleted. I could never get enough sleep, and even the simplest task felt overwhelming. My mood shifted constantly. I was either overeating or barely eating at all.

It seemed like he was the root cause of so much of the physical pain I was carrying. The inflammation, the stiffness, the constant fatigue. But once I left, there was a shift. My body began to reset almost immediately. Oddly, it started with a gastrointestinal issue that lingered for a few days, like my body was purging everything it had been holding onto. Then my sleep improved. My energy returned. I could breathe again. I could *see* again, clearly, without brain fog and anxiety.

I returned to eating healthy and found a sense of peace I hadn't felt in so long.

I learned something invaluable: what I once thought was weakness was my strength. I was so focused on sharing love with someone else that I didn't realize the greatest gift was learning to love and walk with myself. In leaving, I made space for the life and purpose God had planned for me all along, even if it meant continuing forward alone.

✝

"When milk goes bad, it becomes yogurt, richer in flavor and often more valued. If it ages further, it turns into cheese, which is considered even more valuable than both milk and yogurt. Likewise, when fruit sours, it can become wine, something far more prized than the fruit itself. Our mistakes don't make us bad; they shape us. We are constantly evolving, learning, and growing through a humbling process that makes us beautifully, imperfectly human." – unknown

✝

# Anthony

*"You ain't shit and will never be anything thing without me. You will live in the same roach-infested place forever."*

Unfortunately, my response in that moment was, *"Nigga, you are the roach."* I had reached my breaking point. It was not just the absurdity of the accusation, because I have never had a roach in my place, it was the disrespect and sheer delusion behind it. I could not tell if she was confusing me with someone else, she had been involved with or if she had utterly lost her grip on reality. Either way, that moment made it clear: I could never be with someone so toxic and disrespectful.

It was like a lightbulb that had been flickering for months, finally turned on.

This confrontation came after I refused to take her back, despite her many chances to change. She had repeatedly stirred up drama, caused public scenes, and even created false stories to share with family and friends, putting me in difficult and sometimes dangerous situations. Behind closed doors, she would cry and beg for reconciliation.

I did love her. I truly wished we could have built something better together. But the truth is, she was emotionally unstable. There were moments of peace, sometimes weeks, sometimes months, but just when things were going well, the chaos would return. I convinced myself that this was just who she was, that her love came with complexity, drama, and even aggression. I thought I had learned to accept it.

But I was wrong.

She wasn't just difficult, she was destructive. Looking back, I can see how she was chipping away at my sense of self and manipulating how others saw me, all to make herself appear as a victim. Her past relationships followed the same pattern. According to her, she was always the one who got hurt.

Now, I know better. And I am better off for walking away.

# Note

Many men and women are often labeled as narcissists when they may just be carrying deep "mother wounds." Being raised by a narcissistic or emotionally unavailable parent can leave lasting imprints on a child. These early experiences can shape behaviors that resemble narcissism, but they often stem from unresolved emotional neglect, abandonment, and trauma.

For those with mother wounds, the struggle isn't just psychological, it is physiological. The pain becomes embedded in the nervous system, living in the body and shaping how a person responds to the world. Even if someone believes they have moved on from their past, they may not realize how deeply those early wounds have wired their nervous system. This wiring can influence every aspect of life, from how one receives criticism to the kind of partners they choose and how they show up in relationships.

# Couple M

Everything he told her during the six years they shared together, down to every venerable, childhood upbringing, insecurity, mistake, and fantasy she had used against him in a disagreement. From saying things like "you can't buy me a $500 bottle of perfume because you grew up with nothing and don't understand what quality is, or that's why your mother left you and your daddy" she was brutal, cold, and calculated. He loved her in a sick puppy-dog way. Blinded by her beauty and silenced by her compassionate apologies he continued to the relationship. It wasn't that he saw her as a bad person, he knew she was struggling, carrying burdens that weighed heavily on her life. All she needed, he believed, was someone to genuinely love her. He wanted to be that person. He longed for them to be happy together and was willing to show up in whatever way she needed. He even suggested seeing a doctor, wondering if there might be deficiencies or hormonal imbalances behind her pain. His dedication was unwavering; he wanted to face it all together. But she fought him at every turn, pushing him away with harsh words and actions, as if trying to provoke a reaction rather than accept his care. Time eventually wore him down, after all, he was only human. His longing to be loved had slowly been buried beneath the pain of being punished for simply loving her. Numb and hopeless, he began to shut down emotionally.

Ironically, the more distant he became, the more she clung to him. But by then, he had nothing left, not even for himself. He was just drifting, caught in a blank space, depression creeping in like a shadow.

Watching him give up on them terrified her. Quietly, she began making slight changes: scheduling a physical, reaching out to a mental health professional. And in doing so, she discovered that the care she truly needed was more than he could give, but it was exactly what she needed to begin healing and growing.

Meeting him halfway had always been his only ask. And in the end, it became the best thing that ever happened to their relationship.

# A friendly reminder.

Like a demon confined to its den, thrashing in filth and the stench of deception, envy, and torment, Terresa made it her mission to pull others into her personal abyss. Fueled by lies, insecurities, and a twisted boredom, she wove destructive stories that shattered families and severed lifelong friendships, all while wearing the mask of loyalty.

The warmth of a child's smile, a kind gesture, support from loved ones, or the simple joy of a planned vacation, nothing was safe. She poisoned it all with venomous whispers and manipulative lies.

In short, this is about how to recognize a dangerously toxic person, what I call the spirit of the devil.

These people are methodical. They gather your past like ammunition, sniff out your weaknesses, and blend truth with fiction so skillfully it becomes almost undetectable. They build trust over time, disguising manipulation as loyalty, and seek out the emotionally vulnerable, especially those already struggling with jealousy and insecurity. These type of individuals become their easiest prey. When you find yourself sucked into this environment you must call it out when you see it. A person like this can not handle the exposure and they will know instantly where you stand. It is also important to address it on site. Letting it linger is nothing but a green light for them to go plant their seeds of deception on fertile grounds. Being silent and what you think is "the bigger person" or for the sake of friendship is a sign of weakness and access to your time and attention. Being the bigger person comes with great responsibility, being the peacemaker doesn't mean you have to ignore the truth and "stay out of it" truth is your weapon. Intent is your guide. Accountability is the quickest way to slay a person with bad energy. Call it out, verbally or with action and stop it from interfering with your frequency. Remember: we don't need those type of connections and friendship doesn't look like destruction.

# Emeral & Jackson

The apologies, countless apologies were his weapon, and they hooked her every time. Emeral wanted to believe him, to believe in the man he became when he asked for forgiveness. He was gentle in his delivery, sincere in his words, and always seemed to be fighting to recover from the very damage he caused. It was as if he enjoyed the struggle, the more she said no, the harder he would try, with a passion that was almost convincing.

He would do everything right, right up until she gave in, and then it would fall apart, even worse than before.

She came to know him as two different people. One was vulnerable, needing her to feel whole. The other was cruel and controlling, emotionally stuck in a time when being the high school quarterback gave him a free pass for arrogance and immaturity. He would string together weeks of good days, battling against his own trouble-making ego, only to inevitably lose and she would pay the price.

His gifts were grand, expensive, flashy, always bold. It felt like he took inventory of everything she loved, only to use those things later as bargaining chips. She returned to him every time, despite the unhappiness that weighed her down. She convinced herself that this was just part of loving a man.

*"They all have issues, baby. You just have to find the ones you're willing to deal with."*

Her late grandmother's words echoed in her mind. Emeral had been conditioned to make excuses for harmful behavior. That is what women were supposed to do, she thought. As long as a man could provide a comfortable life, wasn't it worth it?

The designer bags, the jewelry, the luxury trips and five-star restaurants, she mistook them for love. They were her love language, or so she thought. So, she chose a battle she believed she could win.

But it ended with a 72-hour stay in the hospital, and a transfer to a mental health facility for further observation.

Everything she believed she had under control had ended up controlling her.

One of the most devastating blows was to her health, her dental health in particular. The stress she carried in silence began attacking her body. Her teeth began to fall out. Painful flare-ups covered her tongue and lips. Specialist after specialist ran tests, only to come back with one word:

**Stress.**

No medical explanation. Just stress, repeatedly. She felt like the doctors used her earlier medical history of the 72 hour hold to write her off as insane.

Her appearance declined until the day she finally left Jackson. Leaving Jackson was just as cloudy as that morning fog; she can recall waking up and deciding to take her own life. she was sure that was the only thing that was going to bring her ease. The constant neglect and non-supportive energy he gave her. laughing and jokes about her doing drugs were the reason for her teeth falling out. His bullying never ended, he was a man that -

Emeral wanted to share what she could of her story, but she couldn't continue, she respectfully asked for it to stop.

If you or someone you know may be having a mental health crisis, please call **911** or walk into your nearest emergency room. Help is available. 95

✝

# Trenton

Trenton stayed with his wife because he loved her, and because his traditional Caribbean beliefs about marriage made separation unthinkable. In their small, close-knit community where everyone knew each other and most were like family there were only two options when facing marital problems: speak to the church pastor or keep it private. Trenton chose silence.

Behind closed doors, he lived a double life. Publicly, he was a loving husband. Privately, he struggled with his wife's dangerous behavior. To the outside world, they were a happy couple, attending church, hosting neighbors, living in a beautiful home. But in truth, he clung to the presence of others, often prolonging outings, or entertaining guests for hours. The more people around, the more his wife resembled the woman he fell in love with. Alone, she became someone else entirely.

She was a secret alcoholic, unwilling to seek help. Her temper flared often, and her words cut deep. Trenton lived under the weight of constant yelling, broken furniture, and shattered glass. He was always repairing walls, replacing windows, or fixing cabinets, casualties of her explosive rage.

Still, he told himself she did not mean any of it. He rationalized her actions, blaming the trauma she carried after losing a pregnancy in the second trimester. When doctors told her she could never have children, it shattered them both. That pain haunted their home like a ghost neither of them could exorcise.

Trenton's way of coping was simply surviving. One day at a time.

He booked group trips as often as he could, sometimes for holidays, sometimes just because. Whether it was a weekend cabin escape or a last-minute flight to somewhere warm, he found joy in planning moments where people could feel connected, free, and full of life. He believed in celebrating everything. Birthdays, anniversaries, promotions, or even just surviving a tough week. Any excuse to gather, to laugh, to make her smile.

When he wasn't planning getaways, he poured his energy into the community. He coached basketball programs for inner-city youth, believing that guidance and consistency could plant seeds of hope. He joined local biking clubs, finding peace in the rhythm of the road and the wind against his face. The gym was his sanctuary, a place where he could release stress, clear his mind, and feel strong when everything else felt fragile.

And on the days when things felt lighter, when her mood lifted or her smile returned, even just for a while he held on to those moments with everything he had. He would take her out to the beach for a quiet walk along the shore, the sound of the waves offering the kind of calm no words could. They would pack a bag and drive out of town for the weekend, chasing a change of scenery, hoping to outrun the weight they carried at home. Sometimes, they would meet up with other couples, laughing over dinner like they weren't holding anything back. In those hours, they looked like everyone else.

But the truth was, none of those escapes could erase what he was carrying. At home, behind closed doors, there were battles that few people saw, the exhaustion, the fear, the loneliness of loving someone through pain they could not always name. He didn't talk about it much. He didn't complain. But it was there.

Still, he stayed.

He loved her not just in words or gestures, but in the way he showed up every day. He carried her pain like it was his own. When others had walked away, grown tired, or given up, he chose to stay rooted. He refused to abandon her like the rest of the world had. His love wasn't conditional. It wasn't romanticized. It was steady, loyal, and sometimes quietly heartbreaking.

He was committed to taking care of her even when it meant putting parts of himself on hold. Even when he didn't recognize the man in the mirror some days. It didn't matter how hard it got, how isolating it felt, or how uncertain the future seemed. For him, love wasn't about ease. It was about presence. And he was there fully, fiercely, and without question.

Because that's what love looked like to him. Not perfect, not painless, but real. And real was enough.

✝

# Mo

She wanted him to prove that the fight he claimed he was willing to wage for their relationship wasn't just words. This time she needed to see him rise after each fall, to face rejection like a Spartan, resilient, relentless, and fueled by a warrior's heart. It wasn't about watching him suffer. She loved him. But she could no longer accept the version of him that had repeatedly hurt her. She refused to carry the burden of his growth. If he wanted to become better, he had to break the old self on his own.

She challenged him, not out of cruelty, but because she saw his potential. She knew the greatness within him, but his fears and insecurities were louder than his desire to evolve, and those fears fed his toxic need for control. He thought a few sweet words could fix everything, like trust could be restored without change. But each time, his promises dissolved into repeated patterns.

Mo had been deeply hurt. His actions didn't just trigger her, they left her isolated, carrying the weight of a relationship that felt more like survival than love. He gave no support, no peace, only pressure, only chaos. It was like carrying the weight of a thousand men who just looked on while she gasp for air. She was suffocating, burned out, depleted.

She knew she couldn't heal in the same place that was breaking her, but her love for him kept her hopeful. No matter the situation he wanted to play both the villain and the hero in her story, not realizing that she was on the verge of something sacred, a spiritual awakening. Something deep inside her cried out for peace, for self-preservation.

Her pain didn't just come from the heartbreak, it came from the dream she had always held close: a love to share, a life built together. Holding the fear that maybe she was meant to do it all alone haunted her. Was she being punished? Or was the kind of love she longed for not even of this world?

Though her body had pulled away, her heart clung to the last fragile threads, waiting for a sign, holding onto something cruel. Something that never showed up in him.

*"Your future is always more rewarding than what's familiar."*

✝

# Dana & Tif

Constantly baiting him was never her fault, at least, not in her eyes. She provoked him into arguments with cruel remarks about his children, his friends, or anything good he had left in his life. That was her way. Toxicity was her language; peace was foreign.

And yet, somehow, their good moments felt strong enough to eclipse the bad. They mistook chaos for chemistry, pain for passion. What started as a fiery dating phase matured into a marriage bound by dysfunction. They became one, but not in the beautiful, poetic sense. They became one in war.

The more she tore him down with her words, the more he began to respond with kindness. Loving her harder changed nothing. The peacemaker inside him slowly died, replaced by the very aggression he once recoiled from. Their home became hostile. His children began refusing visits. His ex-wife filed a court order, citing emotional damage and countless incidents the children reported.

They said their father become someone unrecognizable.

Every day became a firestorm waiting to ignite. Losing weekend visits with his kids isolated him. He felt he had failed them. Their time together was supervised, something he was forced to pay for. It felt humiliating, infuriating. His wife did not care. She didn't want the kids around anyway.

But the pain, his pain screamed inside him every day, even in silence.

That pressure bled into his work, his friendships. People kept their distance. Whispers followed him everywhere. Then one weekend, as he prepared for a visit with his kids, he got a call:

"Today's visit is not healthy for the children. We need to postpone until further notice."

He froze. "What? Why?" he demanded. "How can you decide what's best for me and my children?"

His voice turned into a storm, yelling, cursing at the mediator. He called her names and hung up. Immediately, he called his ex-wife, needing answers, begging for another chance to be with his kids. A father who had never been accused of abuse until now. She didn't answer. He called again. And again. Straight to voicemail.

He knew he had made it worse. Cursing out the social worker would backfire. Anger took over. Instantly, he regretted it, but the rage had already found its home inside him.

He threw his phone into the TV and let out a scream. raw, broken. Tears streamed down his face as his rage boiled over.

Then Tif walked into the room, a smug grin on her face. She had been listening to the entire time.

"What the hell is wrong with you?" she said, chuckling. "Man up. They are just kids. They will get over it."

He sat in silence, head hanging low, her words echoing inside, already drowning in chaos. She turned and walked away, shaking her head.

And that's when he snapped. Information was rapidly connecting at light speed in his brain. "it's all her fault he thought. She is the reason my life has spiraled out of control." What did you say he walked behind her asking. She turned around and repeated what she said but this time with a big smile on her face and laughing as if she had succeeded in making him her inside joke. Without thought, driven by pure anger and frustration he slapped her so hard she stumbled backwards and hit her head on the hallway door. Slightly unconscious as he struggled to keep her awake.

A wave of fear like he had never felt before surged through him. Carefully, he laid her head down and rushed to get icy water, hoping it might help. She lay limp, unresponsive, as he called her name repeatedly, gently tapping her face, desperate for a sign of consciousness. He prayed she would be okay.

Minutes passed, three agonizing minutes, and nothing seemed to work. She drifted in and out of consciousness, a swelling knot forming on her head, darkening in color. Panic rising, he pulled her close, shaking, pleading, "Baby, please wake up."

The thought of calling 911 terrified him but doing nothing was worse. He forced himself to grab the phone and dial for help. His voice trembled as he explained that she had fallen, hit her head, and wasn't doing well.

As he spoke, Tif began to stir, weakly lifting her hand in protest, signaling him to hang up. But he stayed on the line, torn between her wishes and what he knew had to be done.

Afraid but resolute, he finally ended the call and sat by her side, waiting for help. Because of the nature of the emergency, the police arrived along with the paramedics. They assessed her quickly, but she refused to go to the hospital, insisting that she had simply tripped and fallen.

The fear and concern in his eyes must have convinced them, after twenty tense minutes, they left.

He was shaken to the core, disappointed in himself, and haunted by a new, unsettling realization: this moment had opened a door he couldn't close, a door to control, and he wasn't sure he would be able to walk back through it.

Over the next few weeks, he devoted himself entirely to her, catering to her needs, walking on eggshells, and watching her every move. The pressing matter of his children and visitation rights had to be put on hold. He convinced himself it would resolve in time, pushed it to the back burner by necessity. His focus was solely on her now. A new fear had taken root, and he was desperate to navigate it safely.

Tif was happy. She basked in the attention he poured into her, fully aware that she had him right where she wanted. Just the two of them. He became isolated from everything he once held dear, especially his children. He was too afraid to bring them up, too scared of the consequences.

Instead, he lived in a cycle of over-apologizing, pampering her, and begging for forgiveness. As time went on, he noticed that she seemed like a better person, as long as he depended solely on her. There were no arguments, no tension, as long as his children were not mentioned or present. In her version of their life, they simply didn't exist. And in that version, she treated him the way he longed to be treated.

She continued planning their future as though he wasn't already a father. To her, their home was now a "happy home," but to him, it felt hollow, empty without the presence of his children. Still, he stayed silent, fearful of rocking the boat. He hoped time would smooth things over, especially after his last difficult conversation with the social worker. He laid low, convincing himself that twelve months would be enough to set things right.

But time did not fix it. The issue loomed larger until it could no longer be ignored. Eventually, he began sneaking around just to rebuild his bond with his children. One day, he sat down with his ex-wife and poured his heart out, his pain, fears, regrets. He pleaded for a chance to be in his children's lives again.

To his surprise, they began working together in the best interest of the kids. He got creative. He used his PTO from work to plan secret two-week vacations; time he claimed was spent at the office but was really spent with his children. Together, he and his ex-wife reached an agreement: he could visit the children at her house.

Eventually, he secured a small apartment nearby, slowly rebuilding the structure of a healthy life as a father. It was a financial setback, but he knew, deep down, that Tif would never accept this part of him. To her, it was a betrayal. The battle to integrate both parts of his life, his children and his marriage was not only unrealistic, but dangerous. Everything about his world now felt fragile, like it could all come crashing down with one wrong move.

He had planned the weekend while his wife was away on a cruise with her girlfriends. This life, juggling routines, quiet moments, and hidden emotions, had become his new normal. But something about this weekend felt different. Things were about to take a turn.

One evening, his ex-wife came over to the apartment she and the kids had once nicknamed "the safe house." The children had just been tucked into bed when the two of them sat down to talk, something they had not done like this in a long time.

She praised him, acknowledging the dedication and love he had always shown their children, and how, despite everything, they had always been a great parenting team. As the night unfolded, old feelings slowly began to resurface. They spoke openly about their past, how immaturity and pride had led to their divorce. She admitted she wished things had gone differently.

"You were always a good man," she said quietly. "A great provider... a real companion."

She confessed how his current wife seemed to bring out a side of him she never thought existed, a darker, more volatile version. But she respected him deeply for being vulnerable enough to share that truth with her.

He complimented her, asked why she wasn't dating or thinking about remarrying. Her response was swift and honest.

"Because you were the love of my life," she said softly. "And I don't think I could ever share that kind of love with someone else."

Without saying a word, he leaned in and hugged her. They held each other tightly, her hand running through his hair while he gently rubbed her back. The comfort was familiar, safe. They clung to each other until, eventually, they fell asleep in each other's arms.

The next morning, they decided to make it a family day. Together with the kids, they drove a few hours up the coast. It felt like old times, shopping, beachside fun, lunch, ice cream, laughter. He found himself being more affectionate than usual, standing a little too close, brushing her hair back before selfies, noticing the small ways she still moved his heart.

She noticed it too. The chemistry. The quiet pull. Their high school sweetheart energy was still there, vibrating between them like a quiet current. He caught himself gazing at her in thought, still beautiful, still the woman he once loved deeply.

She too, was struggling with the emotions. The night before had stirred something she had tried to bury years ago. Having her family under one roof again, even for a night felt right. She had never stopped loving him, and her thoughts kept circling back to that truth.

As the sun set and they drove back to his place, they both turned to look at the kids' sticky faces, sandy feet, tired but glowing with joy. He reached for her hand, holding it gently yet firmly.

"Thank you," he said, emotion in his voice. "Thank you for letting me have them back in my life. They mean the world to me. And... so do you. You are an incredible woman, and I see that more clearly now than ever."

She smiled, and together, they carried the kids inside and put them straight to bed.

As she made her way to the door, she turned to wish him good night.

"Thanks again," he said, pulling her into one big bear hug.

It was another prolonged embrace, one they both needed. No words, no agendas, just a quiet, real connection. They stood there in silence, holding on to something they were not ready to name, but neither of them could ignore.

She hesitated, not wanting to let go.

"Take care of yourself, okay?" she said softly.

"Good night."

Her head lowered as she turned and walked toward the door.

"Take care of myself?" he echoed, almost to himself.

"I can't do this without you. We're a team, I need you."

He reached for her hand.

She avoided his eyes, voice steady but strained.

"Let's not make this more complicated than it already is."

But when she finally looked up at him, her eyes betrayed her words, filled with longing, with love. Her heart pounded in her chest, heat rising as if something was burning beneath her.

"We need each other," he insisted. "I'm nothing without all three of you. Look at the mess my life has been since we have been apart. Just... stay. Let us figure this out. Together."

He took a shaky breath.

"I'm scared to go back to her. It is killing me inside to live a lie, to deny my children. I cannot keep pretending. I don't want that life anymore."

He looked at her, desperation in his voice.

"Just stay with me tonight. We can talk about anything, everything, until the sun comes up. I need to be with my family."

She let go of his hand, trying not to cry. Her voice was barely a whisper.

"Okay."

They sat out on the balcony, talking for hours, until neither could resist the pull any longer. She stood, walked over to his lounge chair, and lay beside him, resting her head on his chest. With her hand in his, she whispered, "Let's do this… one last time."

Startled, he sat up. Eyes locked.

"Are you serious?" he asked, kissing her hands.

She nodded, tears mingling with her smile.

"Yeah. I love you. I have always loved you. I just want us both to be happy. Promise me… no matter what, we talk. About everything. As long as we keep talking, we will be okay."

They shared one of the most unforgettable kisses of their lives, and we will leave the rest to your imagination.

Dana made the necessary steps to divorce his second wife and remarry his first. It has been seven years since then. They are still going strong. One of their kids just graduated high school, and the youngest has two more years to go. These days, they spend their time dreaming about their empty-nest years and planning for retirement.

Dana reminds himself often: To heal aloud in love, because once upon a time, he nearly lost himself in silence.

# Andy & The Ex

A ndy stood in front of his bathroom mirror, ready to begin the two-week "love yourself" challenge he had seen circulating on social media. But just five minutes in, he realized it was harder than it looked.

*Okay,* he thought. *What loving, positive things do I have to say to myself?*

Nothing came.

Instead, his eyes locked onto every flaw, blemishes, split ends, the fine lines around his eyes, the new streaks of gray in his hair. He barely recognized himself. His face looked tired, skin dull. Heartbroken and emotionally worn he looked like the aftermath of everything he had endured.

His recent breakup had gutted him, but what hurt more was the realization that he had stayed far too long in a relationship that gave him nothing in return, no intimacy, no support, no stability. He had given everything, and still felt alone, both with her, and now, without her.

He took a deep breath and leaned closer to the mirror, summoning the courage to say something, *anything* kind to himself.

"I... I am strong," he whispered.

The words left his lips, but they felt hollow. He did not feel strong. How could he? He had stayed in something that stripped him of his joy, his energy, his sense of self. There had been no reciprocity, no safe place to land, only emptiness disguised as connection.

But even in the silence, he recognized something was shifting. He didn't understand it yet, but he knew something inside him needed to change. Driven to what was familiar, even if it hurt, and now, with nothing left to lean on, he longed for support, something steady to hold.

What he had not yet realized was this: comfort is the enemy of growth. And this version of himself was about to meet, the one who could stand alone, confident and grounded in his own peace, was worth every painful step.

# Will

He always knew the relationship would end eventually. Deep down, he understood that his lack of accountability, refusal to grow, poor communication, and constant disrespect would lead to the same outcome as all his past relationships.

His pattern was predictable: speak poorly about her to others, play the victim, and beg for forgiveness repeatedly, just enough to keep her from walking away completely. And for a while, she didn't. She held on, hoping he would change.

But the things he knew mattered most to her were the very things he intentionally neglected. He thrived on pushing boundaries, it gave him a twisted sense of control. He used the vulnerable things she had shared with him as fuel to justify his harmful behavior. It wasn't love he wanted; it was distance, drama, and chaos.

He introduced problems that were never there before, testing her patience and trust. The disrespect was constant, yet he stayed confident she would always take him back. No real effort, no real change, just empty apologies, and excuses that only brought pain.

His "I love you" was said so often, without meaning or action, that it may as well have been a ringtone. The relationship worked only when she was the one giving, doing, and fixing. He loved how she made him feel, but he had no intention of genuinely loving her back. He was proud of being the whole problem with a destructive relationship history of luring women into his arena of madness.

✝

# Sibel

Of course, he couldn't live without her. But it was never about love. Not real love. It was about survival, a need to anchor himself to something, someone, bright enough to keep his own emptiness from consuming him. She was that light, a spiritual glow he couldn't generate for himself. He didn't want to grow with her; he only wanted to attach himself, like a host that feeds off the flame it envies.

As long as she was there, close enough to control, quiet enough to diminish. He felt powerful. Safe. It was easier for him to belittle her brilliance than confront his own lack. He would shrink her down to his size, ignore the parts of her that radiated out of love, and silence the voice inside her that spoke only of hope and sincerity. And still, she gave.

That was her curse, giving too much to those who had not earned even a piece of her. She poured from her soul as if love was infinite, as if she could bleed without running dry. She didn't just love him despite the chaos; she loved the chaos in him. She saw the wound beneath the bitterness, the brokenness hiding in bravado. And because she was a fixer, she believed she could patch him up with the thread of her loyalty.

She wasn't just trying to heal him, though. That part took time to see. The truth was, she was unconsciously trying to fix herself through him. If she could love someone like him enough, someone incapable of showing up then maybe she wouldn't have to sit with her own pain. Maybe she wouldn't have to face the parts of her that felt unworthy, unfinished, afraid.

Every relationship before him had reflected that same pattern: giving, fixing, sacrificing. Building others from the ground up and calling it love. She wore her empathy like armor, hoping no one would notice it was also her wound. And so, she stayed, even as the cracks in their relationship became chasms.

She stayed when his words turned sharp and his affection went cold. She stayed when he made promises he never kept, grand plans that dissolved at the first sign of effort. Even the smallest commitments, like weekend brunch or a walk in the park, were broken with casual excuses. Yet she always forgave. She told herself he was just overwhelmed, tired, misunderstood.

But the truth lived in the pit of her stomach, whispering every night she cried herself to sleep. He did not forget plans, he disregarded them. He did not cancel because of life; he canceled because he could. And she let him. Because deep down, some part of her believed love meant endurance. That love meant staying, no matter how much it hurt.

The irony was cruel: she gave him everything she never gave herself, compassion, patience, forgiveness. She waited for him to grow into the person she believed he could be, even as he repeatedly proved who he really was. And in doing so, she lost pieces of herself, slowly and quietly. Her laughter faded. Her dreams dimmed. Her boundaries blurred until she could no longer tell where she ended and he began.

Still, she held on, not to him, but to the hope that the chaos would eventually make sense. That if she just gave a little more, tried a little harder, loved a little deeper, it would all somehow work out. She did not realize she was clinging not to love, but to the *familiarity* of the pain. To the idea that suffering had to come before peace. That struggle was the price of worth.

But chaos isn't comfort. It's just distraction. And one day, she woke up exhausted, not from the relationship, but from herself. From always trying to fix what was not hers to fix. From pouring endlessly into people who brought only dust in return. From confusing loyalty with love, and endurance with intimacy.

It did not happen all at once, this realization. It came slowly, an ache that turned into a scream. A moment where she looked in the mirror and did not recognize the reflection staring back. She had become a stranger to herself, molded by someone who couldn't, and simply who wouldn't love her.

So, she let go. Not with rage, not with a dramatic exit, but with strength. She stopped texting first. Stopped waiting for apologies that never came. Stopped explaining her worth to someone who never really saw it. She didn't need closure from him. She needed commitment to herself.

In time, the pressure lifted. The silence that once scared her became sanctuary. The space he left behind was not empty; it was filled with possibility. And in that space, she began to return to herself. She stopped loving people in hopes they would change and started loving herself in ways that reciprocated.

She learned that true love doesn't shrink you. It doesn't ignore your light, it celebrates it. It does not break plans or break you down. It shows up, consistently, quietly, honestly. And most of all, it starts from within.

He, of course, reached out eventually, like they always do. With vague apologies and empty memories, they never cherished. But by then, she had outgrown the cycle. She had nothing left to prove, and nothing left to fix.

She did not hate him. She just finally chose herself.

And this time, she did.

✝

# Don

He sat on the edge of his bed, elbows resting on his knees, hands tangled in his hair like he was trying to hold the weight of his thoughts in place. The silence in the room was so heavy it echoed. His phone buzzed beside him, another message from someone he wasn't sure he wanted to talk to. He didn't even look. He knew the pattern by now.

Another fight. Another apology. Another cold shoulder turning into warm desperation. Then the cycle again. It was familiar, almost predictable.

One toxic relationship after another, and now he was here. Alone. Exhausted. Asking the question he never wanted to face out loud.

**"What is wrong with me?"**

It was not always like this. Or maybe it was, and he just hadn't realized.

He could trace it all the way back to his first committed relationship at nineteen. She had been magnetic, intense, the kind of person who lit up every room, and sometimes, set it on fire. Their passion was undeniable, their chemistry electric. But she also made him feel like he was constantly on trial. If he took too long to reply to a text, she would spiral. If he spent too much time with friends, she would accuse him of not caring. Her love was conditional, and he spent years jumping through hoops to meet those conditions.

When they finally broke up, he told himself it was just her. She had issues. She needed therapy. He needed someone "healthier."

But the second woman came with different traits but the same toxicity. She didn't accuse, she ignored. She played emotional games with a sweet smile, withholding affection and dangling approval just out of reach. He found himself shrinking to fit her moods, trying to be someone more appealing, someone "easier" to love.

Still, he stayed.

He always stayed.

When that relationship ended, he moved on to the next, each one arriving with a different name and face but offering the same emotional instability. At first, he thought he was just unlucky. Then he thought he had a savior complex. But as he stared at himself in the mirror, eyes dull and soul tired, another idea started to creep in.

Maybe it wasn't just them.

Maybe, he played a part in this tune.

He tried to talk to friends about it once. "Why do I always end up with people who hurt me?" he asked during a late-night conversation over takeout and cheap alcohol.

One friend said, "You're too nice."

Another said, "You fall too fast."

A third shrugged. "Maybe you don't love yourself enough."

That one hit like a slap. He laughed it off at the time, but later, lying awake in bed, it echoed louder than anything else.

**Did he love himself?**

**Had he ever?**

He thought about his childhood. His father, emotionally distant, always expecting more. His mother, present, but overwhelmed, loving in her own way but never quite enough to counter the quiet rejection from his father. Praise came sparingly. Criticism arrived like clockwork. So, he grew up thinking love had to be earned, that he needed to be *better,* smarter, calmer, more useful, less needy to deserve kindness.

So that is what he was chasing all along. People who made him feel like he had to work for love, because working for love was the only way he knew how to receive it.

And maybe when someone was kind to him, *genuinely* kind he didn't trust it. He thought they wanted something. Or worse, he thought they were lying. He pushed away the people who treated him well and clung to the ones who kept him guessing.

That was the pattern. That was the trap.

And the scariest part? It wasn't a trap others set for him. It was one he walked into on his own, again and again, like muscle memory, his heart craved it.

He started therapy. Slowly. Hesitantly. The first few sessions, he talked around the problem, joking about exes and calling himself "unlucky in love." But eventually, his voice cracked while describing a moment when one girlfriend screamed at him in the car because he had liked someone's post on social media.

"She said I was cheating," he whispered. "And I started to believe it. I started to think… maybe I was a bad person."

His therapist didn't respond right away. She let the silence hang, then asked softly, "What would you say to a friend who told you that story?"

He opened his mouth. Closed it. Opened it again. "I'd tell them they were being emotionally abused."

"Why can't you say that about yourself?"

Because he didn't want to be a victim. Because being a victim meant admitting weakness. Because if he admitted he was hurt, then he had to feel the pain fully, and he wasn't sure he could handle it.

But he tried.

Over time, he started to see things more clearly. He learned about attachment styles, how his anxious need for approval paired perfectly (and disastrously) with partners who had avoidant tendencies. He learned that "red flags" were not always loud; sometimes they were subtle silences, manipulations dressed as affection, small boundary violations that slowly grew until he had no boundaries left at all.

He learned that love wasn't supposed to feel like walking on eggshells. That needing reassurance didn't make him weak. That setting boundaries didn't make him cruel.

And most importantly, he learned how to be alone.

Alone didn't mean lonely, not anymore.

He started going to the movies by himself. He cooked meals he liked without worrying if someone else would approve. He picked up old hobbies, sketching, running, reading sci-fi novels. He reconnected with friends he had distanced himself from during relationships.

The silence in his apartment stopped feeling oppressive. It started feeling peaceful.

And then something strange happened.

He started attracting various kinds of women.

A woman he met at a bookstore invited him out, not with flirtation, but with kindness. She didn't play games. She replied to texts without delay. She didn't punish him for being vulnerable. When he told her he needed space after a stressful day, she said, "Take what you need."

It was so simple, so ordinary, that it made him a bit uneasy.

His instinct was to sabotage it. To pull away. But he didn't. Instead, he told her about his fear. About his past. About how he was still learning to trust stability.

She listened. Really listened.

And for the first time, he didn't feel like he was waiting for the other shoe to drop. He wasn't anxious. He wasn't chasing. He was just... present.

It was not a fairy tale. There were disagreements. Misunderstandings. But they talked. They repaired. They grew. And even if it didn't last forever, he knew now what he hadn't known before:

**He deserved this kind of love.**

Not because he had changed himself to earn it, but because he had *unlearned* the lie that he had to believe.

Years later, he wrote in his journal:

"I spent so long trying to fix myself for approval so others would love me.

What I needed was to fix the part of me that thought I needed fixing to be loved."

Sometimes, he still wondered what was wrong with him. Old habits die hard.

But now, the question came with compassion. Curiosity, not shame.

"What am I still learning?"

"What do I need today?"

"What part of me needs care?"

And instead of seeking the answer from someone else, he asked himself, and listened.

Not for flaws. Not for faults.

But for the truth he had finally come to believe.

**He was always enough.**

✝

# Yuma

She never imagined that one day she would find herself sitting alone at home, staring blankly at the wall. It wasn't just a casual glance or a fleeting moment of distraction, she was frozen in motion. Time seemed to have stopped around her, as if her body had betrayed her mind and refused to move. She sat there, caught in a strange, paralyzing haze, confused about who she was anymore. Her identity, once so clear and full of hope, now felt like a distant memory, buried beneath layers of exhaustion, pain, and disbelief.

Inside her, faint sparks of fight flickered, tiny bursts of resistance trying desperately to resituate her lifeless body into motion. But the spark wasn't enough, it flickered weakly against the overwhelming heaviness that weighed down her spirit. She was in denial, struggling to accept the reality of her situation. She had been living in a long-term relationship, one that looked perfect from the outside but was, in truth, a cage. Emotionally abused, she had given so much of herself, only to be drained and diminished.

The fight she once had inside her had faded into a dark cloud. Instead of anger or rebellion, she felt only sadness. A deep, aching sorrow that pulsed through her veins. Alongside the sadness came moments of regret and sharp pangs of pain that surged through her body like electricity, jolting her awake, then dragging her back into despair. She wanted to scream, to cry, to break free, but the silence around her was suffocating. She had no one to talk to. No one who could understand.

For years, she had carefully curated the image of her relationship, making it look amazing to everyone around her. She hid the cracks, the bruises, the nights she spent crying alone. To the world, she was happy, strong, and in love. But behind closed doors, she had shut out everyone else. Even her own intuition, all had been pushed away until he was the only one left in her life. He was not just her partner; he was the center of her universe, the sole person she confided in, the only friend she allowed herself to have. It was a lonely, isolating existence.

Her world was shrinking, folding in on itself like a dark, impenetrable bubble. Each day, the walls around her tightened, closing in, suffocating her. She wanted to fight, to push back, to break free, but there was no fight left. Only emptiness, silence, and a feeling of being utterly lost.

She remembered how it had started, trivial things at first. Harsh words disguised as jokes, subtle criticisms that left her questioning herself. Over time, those words had grown heavier, more frequent, more cutting. The emotional abuse wasn't always blatant; sometimes it was a cold silence, a dismissive glance, a manipulation that left her second-guessing her own feelings. Spiritually, she felt drained, as if the vibrant light inside her had been slowly snuffed out by his constant need to control and dominate.

She had tried to hold on, convinced that things would get better. Maybe it was her fault, she thought. Maybe if she changed, if she loved harder, if she gave more, she could save what they had. But love wasn't supposed to hurt like this. It wasn't supposed to drain her until she was empty.

Now, sitting limp in her living room, she wondered where the girl who had laughed easily, dreamed boldly, and loved freely had gone. Was she buried beneath the years of pain, hidden behind the mask she had worn so well? Could she find her way back to herself? The fight to survive had been replaced by a fight to remember who she was.

Her thoughts spiraled, tangled in fear and confusion. How could she trust herself again? How could she reach out when she had told so many lies about her perfect relationship? The shame was a heavy chain around her neck, pulling her deeper into silence. The truth was a secret she guarded fiercely, afraid that if she spoke it aloud, the fragile world she had built would shatter completely.

But somewhere deep inside, beneath the sadness and regret, the smallest spark of hope stayed. It whispered to her in moments of quiet, a reminder that she was more than this pain, more than the abuse, more than the silence. That spark was the seed of her fight, waiting to grow, waiting for her to find it again.

She closed her eyes and took a shaky breath. She didn't know what tomorrow would bring, or how long it would take to heal. But she knew she wanted to try. Even if the road was long and uncertain, even if she had to face the darkest parts of herself, she wanted to find her way back to the girl who had been lost.

In that moment, sitting still but slowly gathering strength, she began to imagine a life beyond the walls of her silent prison. A life where she could speak her truth, where she could rebuild her shattered spirit. A life where she could love herself again.

It would be hard. The fight was not gone, it was just buried, waiting to be uncovered. And, just maybe, this was the first step toward reclaiming her life.

✝

# Tandy & Paul

Anxious from past abandonment and weighed down with guilt, Tandy said, "I do."

At the reception, the atmosphere was lively, guests laughed, music thumped, drinks flowed freely, and compliments poured in. But Tandy stood still, watching Paul, her new husband get so drunk she was unable to enjoy the night herself. Deep down, she knew they were not meant for each other, but after so many years together, it seemed easier to keep going than to start over.

For a moment, her heart pounded in fear. *What did I just do?* But she pushed the thought aside. Married or not, they had already been through so much. They never truly separated, so why not make it official?

But the truth lingered.

Paul had cheated on her for years. He even had a son from one of his affairs, a boy who had just turned thirteen. Paul had begged for forgiveness repeatedly, promising to change. And while Tandy stayed, the emotional toll became a constant trail in her life.

Her thoughts were interrupted by more compliments, "You look beautiful!" and with a forced smile and watery eyes, she offered hugs and hollow thank-you. Every detail of the wedding - the venue, the rings, the dress, his suit, even the honeymoon was paid for by her alone. A total of $185,000, racked up across multiple credit cards, just to present a fantasy to their friends and family.

She hated who Paul really was, so she smiled through it, made excuses, and joined the celebration. By the end of the night, she was just as drunk as he was trying to numb the aching realization that she had married a man she didn't respect.

They were escorted to their room by family. The next morning, they woke up around noon and spent the day at the hotel before flying to their honeymoon. But Paul's phone would not stop ringing. They both knew who it was: his child's mother.

She was relentless, calling nonstop, even reaching out to Paul's brother, who was still at the hotel. When Paul ignored her, she showed up in the lobby, demanding that his son goes with them and to pay her the money he had promised to avoid child support. Her voice echoed through the lobby where family members were having breakfast.

"If you can afford a wedding like that, then you have the money you owe me. I want it today, and I am not leaving without it. If I don't get it, you and your wife are getting hit with child support!"

Humiliated, Paul rushed to the lobby to get her outside. Tandy, furious and deeply embarrassed, stayed in the room, calling his phone, no answer. She finally called Paul's brother, demanding that he bring Paul back before she lost it. Not wanting to make things worse in front of the elders, the brother went to retrieve Paul.

He offered to calm the situation himself and told Paul to return to his wife. Paul agreed, but not before his son was handed off to him.

As Paul turned to leave, the boy's mother shouted, "I don't care if it is your wedding! It's your week. take him on the honeymoon!" Laughing to herself.

Paul glanced back at her, eyes full of contempt. She met his stare with a smirk, her eyes betraying hurt and disgust. She had been sleeping with him up until just a week before the wedding. Heartbroken and bitter, she watched him walk away with their son. With one last eye roll and a cold "F you and your family," she drove off.

Back in the lobby, one of Paul's aunts saw him with his son and stopped him. "No, baby. Don't make things worse. I will take him for the week. Pick him up when you get back from your honeymoon."

Paul, ashamed, handed over his son and returned to the room.

Tandy didn't say a word.

He entered quietly and whispered, "I know. I know. I handled it."

Pulling her close, he kissed her, desperate, pleading and like always, she gave in.

Sex had always been the glue holding them together. Paul had a way of making a woman feel like the only one in the world. It was his weapon, his weakness, and his redemption. No matter how much damage he caused, that part of him lingered seductive, unforgettable. Each time a woman told herself she could separate love from lust just for the pleasure. Each time, they were wrong. he was pure dopamine with a side of cortisol. And she couldn't see how the stress outweighed the pleasure.

It was silly of her to believe that marriage would change his ways. But still, she held on to hope, playing the role of the good wife. She even convinced him to start going back to church with her. For a while, it seemed like things were finally turning around. They got pregnant, he found steady work and had held the job for three years. But by the sixth month of her pregnancy, things began to sour again.

Tandy's pregnancy was a stressful one. She developed diabetes, struggled with high blood pressure, and her weight had become a critical concern to her doctor. Paul, unfortunately, was no support at all. He slowly slipped back into his old ways of flirting with women at work, coming home late, and making cruel, insensitive comments about how he barely recognized her anymore. Her body was changing because she was carrying their child, and yet he dishonored that sacrifice with thoughtless, hurtful remarks.

He was more out of control than ever. Each week, she received anonymous hang-up calls on her cell phone, which was always at night. The signs were obvious, she had seen them before, but she tried to ignore them, clinging to hope and praying that, like before, the storm would pass.

As her pregnancy grew more complicated, her doctor put her on bed rest. Even walking to the bathroom became a challenge. Meanwhile, Paul's behavior grew increasingly suspicious. Though he was physically around the house more often, he spent most of his time downstairs on the phone or out in the garage.

Then, one weekend, Tandy felt better than she had in a long time. She managed to get up, dress herself, and make her way to the bedroom window. Settling into her lounge chair, she looked out and saw Paul in the backyard, assembling a small, colorful playhouse next to a sandbox he had been working on.

She let out a deep sigh and smiled. For the first time in a long while, she silenced the fears he had long dismissed as "insecurities." In that moment, she felt safe, relieved. Despite the jaws of past hurts in her mind, that small act told her he was excited about the baby. Things could actually be getting better.

Paul looked up and saw her watching. He smiled and motioned for her to open the window.

"Do you like it?" he asked.

She smiled back. "It's beautiful."

"Great," he said. "Now get back to bed, I ordered us some food."

Tandy went back to rest, watching movies and eventually dozing off. She woke to the smell of food and Paul bringing in their brunch. That weekend, they shared something they hadn't in a long time, peace. It was one of the best weekends they had had in forever.

As the weeks passed, so did the growth of Tandy's belly. Following the doctor's orders became easier as Paul grew more involved. Although he still held secret conversations downstairs at night, he was more attentive than ever. He brought home baby items, set up the nursery, and added toys and play equipment to the yard, it was starting to look like a daycare center.

Tandy was happy. Her loyalty and dedication to the relationship felt like it was finally paying off. She was ecstatic, spending hours on the phone with her pastor, sharing how Paul was turning over a new leaf. He had finally put his child's mother in her place, and now that she had started dating someone new, she began to respect their marriage.

At eight months, the doctor recommended a C-section for the safety of both mother and child. They scheduled the procedure for the following week, and soon after, Tandy gave birth to a beautiful, healthy baby boy 9 pounds, 5 ounces and 23 inches long.

She and the baby stayed in the hospital for a few extra days due to health concerns but were eventually discharged with doctor's orders for rest. Tandy embraced her new title: mother. She was in love with her son, with her new life, and even with her husband, who finally seemed to be adding peace into their lives.

Two weeks in, the baby was growing and eating well. Tandy, still recovering, moved slowly through the house but was glowing with joy.

One night, Paul called and told her he would be home late and not to worry. Her heart fluttered with a twinge of anxiety, but she pushed it aside as he had been attentive lately. "It's fine," she told herself. "I am overreacting. I need to trust him."

She cuddled with her baby and drifted off to sleep, only to be awakened by a strange noise in the backyard. She told herself it was just Paul, cutting through the yard, or bringing in more items. Expecting the motion light would come on any second. But they didn't.

Her eyes opened wider. She still heard careful, deliberate footsteps. No light. She grabbed her phone and called Paul. No answer. She sent a text:

**"Is that you in the backyard?"**

Still nothing.

Another call. No answer. Another text:

**"Paul, I hear something in the backyard. I'm sure someone is out there. No motion light. Where are you?"**

Still silence.

Tandy crept to a side window. She could hear footsteps but could not see anyone. The motion lights still hadn't triggered. Panic crept in as she felt someone might be watching her. She called him again, no answer. It had been 15 minutes since her last message.

Her heart racing, she dialed 911. The police dispatched a call to the neighborhood security patrol. Security arrived first, slowly circling the property with flashlights. That is when she heard them shouting.

**"Come out with your hands up!"**

Fear gripped her. She tried Paul again, still no answer. She left him a voicemail, voice shaking, telling him what was happening.

Police cars pulled up with sirens and lights flashing. Officers leapt out, guns drawn. A helicopter hovered, its spotlight sweeping across the backyard toward the garage.

Tandy was frozen. She had never been this afraid.

It was like something overtook her entire system. Grabbing her baby, unsure what might happen next, she dropped to the floor, whispering repeatedly:

**"Oh God… oh God…"**

The baby started crying as the noise escalated, dogs barking, officers shouting, the chopper above.

Then, silence.

Her phone rang. It was security.

**"The police have someone in custody,"** the guard said. **"They need to speak with you."**

A loud knock rattled the front door. She crept downstairs, still trembling. Through the peephole, she saw the familiar face of the neighborhood patrol officer. She opened the door slowly.

"Ma'am," one of the officers approached gently, "we have a suspect in custody. However, she claims she lives here."

"My husband!" she exclaimed, cradling her baby tighter. "Paul Wells, that's my husband. I have been calling him!"

The officer raised a hand to interrupt. "Ma'am, the person we have in custody is a female. Her name is Leah Uardds."

Tandy's face twisted in confusion. "No… I, I don't know who that is. It is just my husband and me who live here."

"Is your husband home right now?"

"No, he's at work," she replied, her voice trembling. She gently rocked her baby, now fully aware of the worried eyes watching her. Officers. Security. Neighbors. Everyone was looking at her.

*Who is this woman? What is going on?*

Snapping out of her spiraling thoughts, Tandy walked slowly toward the police car. She peered through the window and saw a young woman, early twenties, visibly pregnant sitting inside.

"I don't know her," Tandy said, trying to make sense of the situation. "Maybe she got confused… Maybe she meant the house next door…"

Silence.

The only sound was Tandy's shallow breathing, growing heavier as panic set in. Confusion. Dread. Fatigue. Nothing made sense.

"Mrs. Wells," a female officer said gently, "please come with me."

She followed, clutching her baby tighter. Several officers and security staff trailed them as they walked toward the backyard. The officer opened the gate behind the clubhouse and led her toward the side of the garage.

When the officer opened the garage door, Tandy's heart skipped.

The space was no longer the unfinished man cave her husband once dreamed of. It was transformed, white and rose-colored decor, a queen-sized bed, a crib, and cozy furnishings. Like a small apartment. Neat. Feminine. Lived in.

The scent of a woman lingered in the air.

Tandy stepped in slowly, her mind spinning, feeling like a stranger in her own home.

"Ma'am," the officer's voice came from a distance, "are you aware someone's been living back here?"

Tandy couldn't answer. Her eyes scanned the space until they landed on a framed photo near the bed.

She walked to it in a trance.

There, smiling back at her, was her husband… and the pregnant woman from the police car.

A sharp, choking sound escaped her lips as she stumbled, clutching the baby. Her knees gave way. An officer rushed forward, gently taking the child from her arms.

"Ma'am? Are you all, right? Can you call your husband?"

Tandy couldn't speak. Her breath came in quick gasps. Her world was crumbling, and she was falling with it.

But somewhere in the chaos, a sliver of strength rose up.

"No," she muttered, then louder: "No."

She stood, mechanically straightening herself. "Give me my baby."

"I don't think that's a good idea, ma'am," the officer said carefully. "We're going to call paramedics, just to make sure you're okay."

"I'm fine!" she said through gritted teeth.

She took her baby back with quiet urgency, then turned and walked briskly toward the front of the house. Neighbors had gathered now. Security exchanged looks of concern and pity. The officers watched her closely waiting for her to break.

But she didn't.

Not yet.

Inside, she shut the door, locked it behind her, then slowly slid down the wall, her baby in her arms.

Rocking. Silent tears were streaming down her face. Her expression was blank yet terrified.

She had no thoughts, just fear. The face of a woman betrayed.

Swallowing the storm of emotions rising inside her, Tandy knew she had to pull herself together, fast. It felt like the police officers were circling, just waiting for her to crack. She shut her eyes tightly, bracing herself shhh… standing up to go put her baby to bed.

Deep breaths through her nose, slow exhales from her mouth, that is what guided her up the stairs. She lay in bed with the baby, frozen, as flashing red and blue lights danced across the ceiling and muffled voices floated through the window. She couldn't move. It was as if her body had shut down, sedating her into sleep just to keep her from breaking.

At 6 a.m., she woke to birds chirping and sprinklers hissing in the backyard. Disoriented, she blinked at the ceiling. It felt like a nightmare. But something was wrong, the baby wasn't in bed with her.

Panic hit like a jolt of electricity.

She jumped up, her breasts aching and leaking. She ran to the nursery. Empty. Down the stairs in a frenzy. Then she saw him, Paul, sitting on the couch, cradling their son in his arms.

"Good morning," he said, voice cracked and rough. "Can we talk?"

She barely managed to find her voice. "Can we talk?" she echoed in disbelief, snatching the baby from his arms and settling onto the couch to nurse. She could not bring herself to look at him. Her body shook with silent sobs until the dam burst crying uncontrollably.

"What is there to talk about?" she gasped. "Who *are* you? What is happening? Who *is* that woman?" Her voice climbed into a scream. "I want you both out! Get out of my house!"

Paul tried to calm her. "Relax. I talked to the police last night. I pulled up and saw everything on the block and…."

She jumped to her feet before he could finish, baby held tight in one arm. She moved to leave the room, and he followed close behind, trying to explain.

And then, before she could even think, she grabbed the candle and swung it at his head, but he dodged it. Looking at her in disbelief, she looks back with hatred. She picks up their wedding picture and throws it. He dodged it again but stumbled and trips on the floor. She stood over him, dizzy and disoriented, watching as he struggled to get up. Without thinking, she turned and ran toward the back door. Pausing just long enough to place the baby in the playpen in the dining room, she bolted to the garage.

She yanked on the door. Locked.

Banging, pulling, kicking, "Open up! Open the door! This is my house! *This is my house!*"

Her voice cracked and softened with each word, drowned by the sudden barking of dogs and the sound of a neighbor moving around their yard. She sank to the ground in front of the door, sobbing.

From inside, she could hear the buzz of cell phone notifications.

Each one made her stomach twist. Each one made her angrier, alone, and in rage. Tandy had not had a chance to mentally connect to what was happening. Her eyes were heavy, but her mind refused to rest. The images, the sounds, the questions, they spun around inside her like a spin cycle.

She walked barefoot to the side of the house, to an old wooden shed where they kept the garden tools. Her hand reached instinctively for the shovel.

The lock on the garage door was fairly new. She jammed the end of the shovel under it, yanking hard. The metal clanked loudly, echoing off the silent street, but she didn't care. Her only focus was getting inside.

The banging continued, metal against metal, frustration against steel. Every swing of the shovel was fueled by thoughts she couldn't hold. Who was this woman living in her garage? How long had she been there? Was she pregnant with her husband's child?

The thought made her skin crawl.

Paul.

The name used to taste sweet in her mouth. Now it was sour, bitter, like something spoiled. He had promised her so much, given her so little, and now this.

"Why?" she murmured under her breath. "Why would you do this to me?"

Her grip tightened on the shovel as she slammed it harder against the lock. The garage rattled with each blow. Her arms ached, but her mind was louder than her body's cries for rest. Sweat slid down her back. Her breath came in ragged gasps. She didn't notice Paul until his hand closed around the handle of the shovel.

"Tandy, stop!" he shouted, pulling it from her grasp.

She turned to face him, wild-eyed and trembling. Her voice cracked from screaming but still came out sharp.

"How could you do this to us?!" she screamed. "Who is she, Paul? Is she pregnant with your baby? Why are you like this?!"

Paul took a step back, stunned, even ashamed. But shame wasn't enough. She needed answers. She needed truth. She needed her life not to be unraveling right in front of her.

"I hate you," she said. The words dropped like lead between them. "I hate you."

Tears filled her eyes, but they were not soft or delicate. They were violent, stinging, full of rage and heartbreak. Her knees wobbled beneath her, and she pressed herself against the garage door for support. Her breasts ached, filling with milk, a cruel reminder that her child was still inside the house, needing her.

She was still a mother.

A woman who needed to survive, if not for herself, then for her child.

"Get out of my house," she whispered, her voice barely audible. Then louder, "GET OUT. Both of you. Just go… go to hell."

Her words hung in the thick air. She turned and walked back toward the house, shoulders hunched, her entire body sagging under the weight of betrayal. She didn't look back.

Paul stood frozen. A man wrapped in lies, now choking on them. He had told the woman in the garage that he owned the house, that he inherited it from his deceased parents. He said he was completing his divorce, that Tandy was just the last legal hurdle before they could be together. She believed him. She had to, he made her believe and the poor woman was in desperate need.

And now she was pregnant, too.

Four hours. That's how long Paul stayed in the garage, trying to explain, trying to calm her. The pregnant woman, Leah, sat on the bed, clutching her belly and asking over and over again, "What's going to happen to me?" She was young, naïve, and about to become a seasoned woman.

He had no answers. Only regrets.

Back inside the house, Tandy sat in the nursery rocking chair, feeding the baby, the silence pressing down on her chest. She felt like a stranger in her own home. She wanted to scream as loud as she could to release some of the pressure, but she didn't. She was too tired. Too broken.

She looked down at her child, so innocent, he paused from nursing and smiled at her as if reminding her: *I'm here. I need you.*

Paul was not going to change. He never had. The apologies, the soft voice, the empty promises, he used them like weapons, and she fell for them every time.

Not anymore.

Not after this.

She grabbed her phone and stared at the screen for a long time before finally pressing the contact: *Mom.* Her thumb hovered over the call button. For years, she had shut out her family. Paul made sure of that. Made her feel like they did not understand, like he was the only one who genuinely loved her.

But he didn't love her.

Not really.

She pressed the button.

"Hello?"

Her mother's voice cracked with surprise.

"Mom," Tandy said, her voice breaking. "I need help."

Paul eventually left. Not completely, but he left the garage, took Leah to a motel across town. Promised her it was temporary, promised he would fix everything.

He was still making promises.

Tandy didn't know what would happen next. She didn't know how long the pain would last, or if she would ever be able to forgive herself for staying with him as long as she did. But she knew one thing: she had to get out.

Two weeks later.

Her mother helped her pack up his things and change the locks to the house and garage door. Her sister brought her food to make sure she was eating enough for herself and to produce milk at such a stressful time. Old friends, the ones she had ignored for years, sent texts, asked how they could support her they helped her set up cameras in the back yard, and even spent nights there with her hoping he was going to bring Leah, back around. Everyone who found out was angry and willing to help her. Slowly, the pieces of her life that he had chipped away started to feel supported.

Paul had the audacity to send a text letting her know when the baby was born, and that they named him Isaac, as if he was expecting her to congratulate him. He sent messages after messages, like they could work on being friends. He even showed up once, asking to see the baby, asking for another chance.

Tandy didn't open the door, only because her mom had been staying there for months, helping out with the baby but things had starting weighting on her, she started feeling sorry for Paul, his messages were full of the usual stories of how the world cursed him and she was the only place where he felt peace. Deep down, she needed to feel needed from him and just wanted the pain to stop.

She had convinced herself that she could slowly forgive him and at least co parent. Her mom begged her not to allow him a chance to creep back into her life, her friends pleaded and tried to keep her distracted with group events and support. Her dad rolled in his grave for 15 months up to the day she let him back in the home "for the sake of their son." Her mom and friends were disappointed but stayed supportive. They realized that there was something deeper going on with her and did not want to lose her They were concerned she was on the verge of a nervous breakdown and wanted to stay close this time. so, they learned to find a non-judgmental space in their marriage.

Everyone but her could see Paul, for the man he was two children from cheating on her and one they had together, Tandy was the only one holding things down, she had the money making career while he struggled to keep jobs, everything was in her name, the car he drove, insurance and authorized user on her established credit cards where she had to look at purchases on her statement funding his foolishness, from taking women out on dates to co pays for the new child's doctor visits was always a projection on her.

Her sleepless nights, depression, countless tears, the disrespect, his serial cheating and emotional abandonment were ongoing. She wanted better but, didn't believe she could weather the storm within to get to sun and sandy days she wanted with him. she put it all on "staying in the marriage for their son but knew one day he would see his father for who he was, and either be just like him or grown to hate him for the pain he caused his mother. It would reach a point where their son would have questions about his two half-siblings and see for himself. This would be his example of a man, of a father, and of a marriage.

Today, they are still married and living a social media life of happiness while struggling in a reality of pain, where he would eventually destroy her financially. He no longer holds a job and has two separate child support cases for the next eighteen years.

She knew he was a train wreck, but like she told a friend once, "he's, my wreck."

# Bev & E

It was always *later* with him. The time he gave her, those fleeting conversations, and brief indulgences, were never quite enough. She had a fierce, lionhearted love to offer, and he was the only one she wanted to give it to. Others had come and gone, some even stayed a while, but none could match the connection she felt with E.

He knew she was obsessed with him, and that awareness made him comfortable. But the downside to it all was the distance and availability. She had grown numb to his restrictions, to the role he kept her in, always waiting, always second. Still, the ache of wanting him pulsed through her like a drug she never asked for.

Their relationship was a patchwork of postponed plans and text messages; a life suspended in limbo. But even with all the delays, she couldn't picture her world without him in it. So, they always stayed in touch. She had once again gone off grid because she moved on to feel love, but not a day went by that she was not thinking about him.

One random Sunday morning:

**E:** "Wyd?"

**Bev:** *Wow… I was just thinking about you. Long time. I just got married to Dwight, I don't know if you remember him, but we all went to school together. He was a grade ahead of us. Anyway, we moved to the islands. Just got back from a morning hike. What's new with you?*

**E** "Oh, you know… same old, same old."

Disappointed with her reply, he struggled with what to text next. No congratulations, what's your husband's name again? …. Is what she looked at on her phone, and then, nothing. Radio silence, for a year. It was easier for him

Conflict made him uncomfortable. Because he thought ignoring emotions was the same as handling them. So, he buried them deep, lets them rot, then forces himself to eat the spoiled leftovers later.

Eventually, he called. Looking for answers.

But by then, she was divorced. And honestly? Didn't care much about his feelings or any man for that matter.

She still held a special place for him. but now slightly bitter. he was the reason she was constantly searching for that person and looking for somewhere to settle down in life with a partner. She made bad decisions and welcomed people in who would never measure up to him, never satisfying what she yearned for.

E had always been her peace. He was the man of the hour but always missed the minutes that mattered. Their call was real and unexpected. Catching up was always on his timeline. I got married, because of you. She spoke. you put me on hold for so long. I never wanted anyone but you. reminding him of their last serious conversation.

Remember you texted this to me two years ago. To his surprise she sent him a screen shot she had saved in her photos.

**Bev:** *I could love you like this forever. Real, true, loyal. I just needed a few slight changes.*

**E:** *"I cannot give you more than what I am already giving. I have nothing left to offer."*

**Bev:** *Fighting back her pain and wanting clarity. She just replied: Message received.* You have said it for the third time, and I finally believe you. ok, I get it.

"And with that I had moved on."

Surprised that she still had that message and it had impacted her so strongly he said: I know. That was then. This is now.

They were older now, he was done raising his children, with nowhere else to be, no games or practices to run to. No homework, dinners, or college preparatory events to attend. He was available and she was always willing. Where are you he asked. I am coming to see you. Without hesitation, she gave him her location. Twenty minutes later, he texted her confirmation of his flight and said: I will see you tomorrow night, ok? And, ok she replied.

The next night he landed and decided not to call her and took a taxi, as soon as he arrived at her beautiful beachfront property, she opened the door looking at him like it was just yesterday. A big smile on her face, they embrace. His hugs felt the same, his kiss was just as magical as it had ever been. spending the next 3 weeks in each other's arms. Enjoying what they could finally call a life together. So, what do we do? she asked, spend what is left of our lives looking back.

Knowing it could've all been different. Better. If only we had not wasted decades stuck in the same cycle you started, with just a few small words?

Now here we are old. Still tangled up in each other.

Still carrying heartaches and triggers that never had to be ours, if you had only been brave enough to love me the way I needed.

Laying on his chest, he looked at her and said, what he always had said. "Nothing has changed for me." I love you today just as much, if not more than I did thirty-five years ago. I am here like I have always been, and I am here to stay. And just like that. No questions asked. No grudges held. No egos to babysit. The two spent the rest of their lives the way they were afraid to live it together earlier on.

# Owen & Issy

Owen and Issy were born into the spotlight. From an early age, they knew no silence, no privacy, no room to breathe without a camera flash or whispered judgment trailing after them. Fame had found them before they had even found themselves. By the time they met, both had already learned how heavy the world could feel when it was constantly watching, constantly demanding, constantly taking.

But when their eyes met for the first time, backstage at a charity gala neither of them had wanted to attend, it was as if the world paused. Just for a moment. In that brief flicker of time, nothing else mattered but the recognition in each other's eyes. Two individuals that had been wandering in separate storms had suddenly found shelter.

Owen was known for his music. His voice had been called haunting, ethereal, the sound of a generation. But behind the lyrics and melodies was a quiet boy with a soft heart, who never quite felt at home in the glittering, relentless world he had been thrust into. Issy was an actor, beloved for her roles in films that made people cry, laugh, and feel. But beneath the red carpets and rehearsed smiles was a girl who just wanted to be held without expectation.

They found in each other what the world never gave them: honesty. Safety. A place where masks could be taken off and they could just be Owen and Issy, not *Owen Harrow, the voice that made us weep* or *Issy Lane, Hollywood's girl.*

They loved hard. Fiercely. With a kind of devotion that made the earth tilt slightly when they were in the same room. People noticed it, of course they did. And the world, hungry and never satisfied, latched on.

At first, the attention felt like validation. Magazine covers, social media tributes, fan accounts declaring them the modern Romeo and Juliet. But the praise turned quickly. Rumors twisted their bond into drama. Jealousy soured admiration. Strangers picked apart their smiles, their outfits, their body language. The love that had once felt like refuge became a battlefield where they had to defend their right to simply care for one another.

"It's like they want us to fail," Issy whispered one night, curled up beside Owen on the balcony of their shared apartment. The city lights below shimmered, mocking their attempts at peace. "They watch us like a show, waiting for the ending."

Owen did not reply. He didn't have to. His hand reached for hers, squeezing gently, and in that quiet space between them, his silence spoke louder than words ever could.

They tried to fight it. Tried to hold onto the joy that had once lit them up from the inside out. But fame is a cold thing, and the world, when it turns cruel, can sink its teeth in deep. Paparazzi followed them even on their worst days. Tabloids invented betrayals and breakdowns. People on the internet, safe behind anonymous screens, threw insults like stones.

The weight of the world grew heavier.

Issy began to withdraw. The sparkle in her eyes dulled, her laughter came less often. Owen kept writing songs, pouring every ache and hope into his lyrics, but even music began to feel hollow. They were still together, but the joy had been bruised. Their love remained, unwavering, but love, no matter how strong, sometimes isn't enough to silence the world.

One evening, after another headline questioning Issy's mental health and another round of vitriol about Owen's latest single, they sat on the floor of their living room, surrounded by unopened mail and dim candlelight. The air felt too thick to breathe.

"I feel like I'm drowning, O," Issy said, voice barely above a whisper. "And everyone's watching me struggle, cheering it on."

He reached for her, pulled her into his arms. "I know. I feel it too."

They cried that night, not for themselves, but for the peace they had never been allowed to keep. For the life they had wanted to build but kept getting torn apart. For the home they dreamed of, not made of walls and furniture, but of silence, freedom, and the simple act of existing without being seen.

"I just want to be somewhere quiet," Issy murmured.

Owen nodded. "With you."

They spent the next few days like a dream. They went to the beach at dawn and watched the waves with salty air brushing their faces. They danced barefoot in their kitchen to old records. They talked for hours about life, love, the pain of being alive when the world demands your soul as payment for your gifts.

And then, one morning, the world woke up to silence.

Two notes were left behind, one in Issy's handwriting, one in Owen's. They were addressed not to the public, not to the press or their fans, but to each other.

*"You are the only place I ever felt free,"* Issy wrote. *"If this is the only way we can live in peace, then let it be somewhere the noise can't reach us."*

*"They don't get to define our ending,"* Owen's note said. *"We choose it. Together. Always."*

The news hit like thunder. Shock turned to outrage, mourning turned to blame. Debates filled the airwaves. Were they selfish? Were they victims? Who should have seen it coming? Who failed them?

But none of the noise mattered anymore. Not to Owen and Issy.

They were finally somewhere quiet.

In time, their story became more than tragedy. It became a conversation. About pressure. About mental health. About the impossible weight of being human under a spotlight that never turns off. Statues were never built, but songs were written, and movements sparked in their names. People remembered how they looked at each other, how they loved so openly, so honestly, despite the ugliness around them.

And, just maybe, their choice, while devastating, opened a path for others to speak up, to reach out, to demand a gentler world.

A world where love like theirs didn't have to hide or suffer.

A world where quiet could be found while still alive. RIP

*Owen & Issy... We love you.*

*"Your journey is yours alone, no one else is meant to walk it with you. The people we meet along the way often serve as mirrors or tests, helping us see what we've truly learned."*

✝

*"Imagine hurting the person God sent to heal you."*

✝

# Al & Layla

Al sat quietly in the softly lit office of his therapist, the air thick with unspoken words. He had been coming here for several months now, peeling back the layers of a life that, for too long, he had chosen to suppress. His childhood, marked by absence, emotional neglect, and the unhealed wounds of abandonment, had shaped him into a man who often ran from intimacy, but clung desperately to connection, even when it was destructive. Therapy had opened a door he hadn't realized was locked: the door to accountability.

Each session pulled a little more truth out of him, like extracting splinters embedded deep in scarred skin. And as the weeks passed, Al began to feel that he could no longer carry the weight of his own silence. His therapist didn't push him; he merely offered questions like mirrors. And one of those questions had changed everything: *"Who would you be without your secrets?"*

That question haunted him.

There was one secret, particularly that churned in his stomach like acid. It was not just a matter of betrayal; it was the way it collided with the very foundation of his present life. He had been unfaithful to his partner, Layla, for over two years. The affair had ended months ago, but the shame stayed. The worst part? It had not been a fleeting, meaningless lapse, it had been with someone they both knew, someone Layla trusted deeply.

Sierra.

She wasn't just Layla's friend; she was the godmother of their daughter, Mia. That fact alone made the entire situation grotesque to him now. At the time, he told himself the usual lies, that he was lost, that Sierra offered understanding he couldn't find elsewhere, that it wasn't serious. But over time, the duplicity of it all poisoned his sense of self. Ending the affair had given him no peace. If anything, it intensified the guilt.

Layla was no fool. She had noticed the shift in his energy months ago. Al could feel her watching him at dinner, could sense the way her questions had become more loaded. She never outright accused him, but trust had begun to erode in small, sharp ways, long silences, late-night arguments about nothing, her eyes narrowing every time Sierra's name came up in conversation.

Al had convinced himself she did not know. He still clung to that hope. But deep down, he feared that one day, Sierra might tell her out of guilt, or worse, spite. That fear wasn't about saving himself anymore. It was about control. He wanted to be the one to tell Layla, not because he expected forgiveness, but because she deserved the truth from him. And because, after everything, he still loved her.

Therapy made one thing clear: healing could not coexist with deceit. And so, Al made the hardest decision he had ever made. He would confess.

The evening, he chose to tell her was painfully ordinary. They had just put Mia to bed, the lullabies still echoing faintly through the baby monitor. Layla was in the kitchen, rinsing dishes, her back turned to him. Al sat at the edge of the couch, hands clasped between his knees, rehearsing the words he had practiced in front of a mirror for days. Nothing seemed sufficient.

"Layla," he said, his voice cracking just enough to get her attention.

She turned, drying her hands with a towel, eyebrows raised slightly in curiosity. "Yeah?"

He motioned for her to sit. She hesitated, sensing the weight of the moment, then joined him, folding her legs beneath her.

"There is something I need to tell you," He began. "And I need you to let me finish before you say anything."

Layla nodded slowly. Her face had already shifted. She knew. Or at least, part of her did.

"I have not been honest with you. For a long time. And before I say anything else, I want you to know that I am not saying this to hurt you, I am saying it because you deserve the truth. And because I need to live in the truth, no matter what it costs."

Her expression tightened.

"I was unfaithful to you," he said. "For over two years."

Layla did not flinch. She stared at him, her silence both a wall and a wound.

"It was… with Sierra."

That name hit like a grenade.

She stood up abruptly, hand over her mouth. "No," she said, shaking her head. "No, no, no…"

"I ended it," Al said quickly, standing now too. "Months ago. I swear to God. It is over. It should never have happened. I was lost; I let myself believe things that were not true. And I hate myself for it."

Layla was crying now. Not the loud, angry kind of cry, but the slow, stunned, unraveling kind. Her pain filled the room like smoke.

"With *her*?" she said, voice breaking. "Mia's godmother? My *friend*?"

"I know," Al said. "I know how bad this is. I live with it every day."

She turned away, pacing. "You let her hold our child. You let her stand next to me and smile like nothing was wrong. And you… you lied every single day."

"I know," he repeated, his own eyes stinging. "I am not asking for anything. Not forgiveness. Not understanding. I just… I could not live with the lie anymore."

Layla laughed bitterly through tears. "You couldn't live with it? What about *me*? What am I supposed to do with this?"

"I will leave if you want me to. I'll do whatever you need. I just couldn't keep pretending."

Silence fell again, stretching painfully between them.

"Why now?" she finally asked.

"Because therapy made me realize something. I can't become the man I want to be if I keep hiding the man I have been. I have hurt you, and I don't know if there is any fixing that. But I need to stop running from who I am. For me. For Mia. For you, even if you never want to see me again.

The days that followed were excruciating. Layla moved into the guest room. Sierra was blocked from everything, calls, texts, social media. As Layla took the time to mourn the loss of what she believed was her friend. Al stayed in the house, per her reluctant permission, only because they needed to navigate co-parenting. But he kept his distance.

He returned to therapy with a different kind of urgency, no longer seeking answers, but rather the strength to live with the consequences of his choices. Some days, he wondered if he had made a mistake in confessing. But deep down, he knew that truth was the only way forward, even if that forward meant walking alone.

Over time, Layla's anger became colder, more measured. The fire faded, replaced by something harder to bear: indifference. She still loved him; he could see that in the way she sometimes looked at him when she thought he wasn't watching. But the trust was shattered, and love without trust was just a memory of something beautiful.

Al didn't beg. He didn't plead. He simply stayed present. He showed up. For Mia. For therapy. For the quiet process of rebuilding a life that had imploded.

Months passed. Slowly, awkwardly, they learned to coexist. They had long, painful conversations about co-parenting, about boundaries, about the possibility of healing. Layla didn't offer reconciliation, but she did begin to offer something again. A warm nod, a shared laugh over something Mia said. Tiny flickers of connection in the ashes of what once was.

Al knew he might never win her back. But that was no longer the point. The point was to be a better man than he had been, to be honest, even when it hurt; to be accountable, even when it cost him everything.

And maybe, one day, when Mia was old enough to understand, he could tell her the truth too, not about the affair, but about the power of facing your flaws, and the courage it takes to change.

Until then, he would keep doing the work. One truth at a time.

✝

*"Forgiveness doesn't always look like before."*

✝

*Sometimes, repeatedly hurting someone you love is just a misguided attempt to protect yourself.*

✝

*"The weight of life's gentle moments can sometimes leave the biggest scars."*

✝

# Nora

Nora watched the raindrops trace lazy patterns down her apartment window. They moved like thoughts. Slow, heavy, pulled down by gravity. She wrapped her sweater tighter around her and sank into the couch, a book open in her lap but untouched. Outside, the city hummed, but inside, it was quiet. Too quiet.

The phone buzzed again.

Leo.

She didn't pick it up.

Not yet.

He had called twice yesterday. Left a voicemail the day before that. Said he was thinking about her. That he missed their walks. That she didn't have to say anything, he just wanted her to know.

And she believed him. That was the problem.

Nora had never doubted his sincerity, not once. Leo was the kind of person who asked how your day was and meant it. Who remembered your favorite author and left used copies of their books in your mailbox. Who noticed when your hands trembled over dinner and didn't ask why, just gently took them in his own.

But love, for Nora, was complicated. Love came wrapped in barbed wire. Tied up in memories she didn't ask for and flashbacks she couldn't control. When she was fifteen, she had learned what it meant to trust the wrong person. When she was twenty, she learned that apologies don't undo bruises. And by the time she was twenty-seven, she had built walls so high that no one, not even herself, could see past them.

Now thirty-two, she was learning something even harder: that healing wasn't about forgetting, it was about surviving and still choosing to love.

But that choice terrified her.

Because she didn't trust herself not to hurt people.

She didn't raise her voice. She didn't throw things. She didn't say cruel words, she did not mean. But she shut down. She left messages unread. She apologized too often or not at all. She clung too tightly or pulled away the moment someone reached for her.

And Leo? He was patient. But she knew patience had its limits.

She wasn't afraid of him hurting her.

She was afraid of becoming the one who would hurt him.

They met at a used bookstore on 5th Avenue, over a shared copy of *Letters to a Young Poet*. He had smiled. She had flinched. But he didn't push. He asked if she liked Rilke, and when she said yes, he said, "Me too," and walked away. No number. No pressure. Just a moment.

That, more than anything, was why she continued to go back to the bookstore until the connected again. They exchanged numbers and a week later she called.

From the beginning, Leo never asked for more than she could give. He didn't press when she pulled back or wanted to avoid loud bars. He asked questions gently and accepted it when she shook her head.

"I'm still learning," she had told him, after a panic attack left her curled up in his kitchen, sobbing over spilled tea. I know I have issues and I'm trying.

"I know," he had said. "I'm still here."

And that's what made it unbearable.

Because how long could someone stay when you didn't know how to let them in?

Nora had spent years studying trauma. Not formally, no degrees or dissertations. Just quietly, in books and late-night articles and the margins of self-help workbooks she never finished. She knew all the buzzwords: avoidant attachment, hypervigilance, emotional flashbacks. She could list symptoms like a doctor and still couldn't name the thing clawing at her chest at 2 a.m.

But one word kept coming back to her, again: *shame.*

It was shame that curled her spine when Leo said, "I love you" and she couldn't say it back. Shame that made her flinch when he reached for her hand in public. Shame that whispered she was broken, and worse, dangerous.

Because what if she pulled him into the same darkness she fought to escape?

What if her trauma became his?

"I think I'm scared of hurting you," she confessed once, during one of their long, quiet walks through the arboretum. The leaves were turning. Amber, rust, gold, everything fragile and beautiful.

Leo didn't look surprised.

"I know," he said.

"And you're not scared of that?"

He thought about it. "Sure. But I'm more scared of you never trying."

That answer stayed with her for weeks.

She thought about it while brushing her teeth, while stirring soup, while curled up with her cat in bed. What would it mean to *try*? Not to fix everything. Not to be perfect. But to show up, messy and scared, and still reach for someone.

She had spent her whole life protecting others from her pain. But maybe healing meant letting people decide for themselves whether they could carry it with her.

The third time Leo called that week, she answered.

She didn't say much. Just listened. Let his voice fill the silence like light slipping under a closed door. When he asked how she was, she paused before answering.

"I'm not okay," she said.

"That's okay," he replied.

And something loosened.

Therapy helped. Slowly. Painfully.

Nora started going every Thursday at 3 p.m. Dr. Alvarez was soft-spoken and firm, which Nora needed. She didn't let her deflect with humor or vague metaphors. She pushed. Gently. Persistently.

"You're not a danger to people just because you're hurting," she said one session.

Nora had looked away.

Dr. Alvarez continued, "You have internalized the idea that your trauma makes you unsafe. That's not true. What you're really afraid of is being vulnerable."

That word again.

Vulnerable.

She hated it.

But she also wanted it.

Because vulnerability was the space where love lived. And for the first time in a long time, she wanted to live there too.

Over time, she started opening up. Bit by bit. Like unfolding a letter she wasn't sure she had the courage to read.

She told Leo about the years she could not remember clearly. The time she hid in a library bathroom for three hours to avoid going home. The night she called a crisis line and didn't speak, just listened to the counselor breathe until she calmed down.

He didn't flinch. Didn't offer pity. Just listened.

And when she was done, he held her hand. Not tightly. Not as an anchor. Just enough to say, *I'm here.*

They didn't become perfect.

There were still nights when she disappeared into herself, and mornings when she apologized for it.

There were arguments, real ones. Where she wanted to run and he wanted to fix things, and they had to meet somewhere in the middle.

But she stayed.

And so did he.

And one day, sitting across from him at their favorite coffee shop, she looked up from her tea and said, "I love you."

It wasn't grand or dramatic. It didn't fix everything.

But it was real.

And for Nora, that was enough.

Sometimes, she still had dreams. The kind where her past crept back in like fogs under a door. But now, she talked about them. Sometimes with Dr. Alvarez. Sometimes with Leo. Sometimes just with herself, over a cup of coffee and a sunrise.

She no longer believed healing was a destination.

It was a series of choices. To breathe. To stay. To try.

And most of all, to love, even when it was hard.

Because love, she realized, wasn't about perfection.

It was about presence.

✝

# Gail & Robert

It had been twenty years since Robert and Gail stood before friends and family and promised to walk through life together. Back then, they were full of hope, like most newlyweds. They were young, full of ambition, and still charmed by each other's flaws. But time has a way of wearing the shine off things, and for Gail, that charm had long since given way to something darker.

In the early years, Robert was sharp, charismatic, and driven. Promotions came swiftly, opportunities opened, and the admiration from others followed. To friends and family, Robert became a success story, someone who had made good on his potential. Gail was there too, of course, but she was often seen more as the wife of Robert than as Gail in her own right. And that stung.

At first, it was subtle: a passive-aggressive comment here, a jab at his jokes there. When he talked about his work or shared a story at dinner, Gail would roll her eyes just slightly, or chuckle in a way that undercut him. But over time, those tiny things grew sharper, more deliberate. She found ways to criticize him in front of others, correcting him on minor details, questioning his judgment, pointing out things he had forgotten. All of it cloaked in humor, sarcasm, or concern.

But it wasn't funny. And it wasn't really concern.

Somewhere along the way, Gail had become jealous, not of Robert's success itself, but of how people *saw* him. He was respected. Admired. Listened to. And that gnawed at her. Especially because, in private, she held on to the early days when he made *her* feel small, without even trying. A careless joke, a comment he forgot he made, or simply his confidence in contrast to her own self-doubt, it had planted a seed of resentment. And over the years, she watered it.

She never forgot how she had once stood next to him at a dinner party, just months into their marriage and he had told a story about her disastrous attempt at cooking for his parents. Everyone had laughed. Even she had laughed. But inside, it felt like something broke. He didn't mean to humiliate her, but in her mind, he had. And she never let go of that feeling.

Now, after twenty years, every gathering became a battleground, even if only she could see the war. She interrupted him when he spoke, contradicted his memories, pointed out his faults, always with a smile that said "I'm just being honest." But the intent was clear to anyone paying attention: she wanted to bring him down a peg. Especially when family was around.

At Thanksgiving, she would say things like, "Oh Robert loves to *pretend* he does the dishes," or "You know how he is; he always has to be the smartest one in the room." At birthday parties, she would laugh and say, "He acts like he raised the kids. Don't let him fool you, he barely knew their teachers' names."

Robert didn't always fight back. Sometimes he ignored it, smiled politely, changed the subject. Other times, the tension bubbled up and arguments followed them home. But what was hardest for him wasn't the public embarrassment. It was the slow, grinding realization that the woman he had married no longer respected him, and hadn't for a long time.

It wasn't that Gail was unkind in every moment. She could still be warm, still make him laugh when no one else could. She remembered birthdays, worried when he was sick, and still made him coffee on Sunday mornings. But there was an edge under all of it, a bitterness that never truly went away.

In her quiet moments, Gail might not have admitted to jealousy. She saw herself as the realist, the one who saw through Robert's charm and made sure his ego didn't get too big. Maybe, in some corner of her heart, she thought she was protecting him, from himself. Or she just couldn't forgive the way life had unfolded, the ways she felt overlooked, outshined, and misunderstood.

But Robert had noticed. So had others.

Friends who used to admire their dynamic now shifted uncomfortably during conversations. His siblings, once fond of Gail, began to ask if everything was okay. Even their kids, now nearly grown, had started to pick up on the undercurrent, those sharp little exchanges that didn't feel quite like teasing anymore.

And Robert? He had changed too. There was less laughter in his voice now when Gail poked fun at him. He spoke a little less around her friends and stayed longer in the garage when they hosted dinners. He was not angry, exactly, more tired. Worn out from years of subtle digs and public put-downs. There were moments he still loved her deeply, but also moments he mourned what their marriage had become.

He sometimes wondered: had she ever really been happy for him? Or had it always been a competition she never signed up for, but couldn't stop playing?

And Gail, for all her sharpness, had moments of quiet too, when she watched him from across the room and saw the lines on his face, the weight he carried, the way he stayed silent when once he would have spoken up. Maybe she knew what she was doing. Maybe she hated herself for it. Or maybe she believed it was justice, payback for all the invisible ways he had made her feel small.

But the sad truth was this: what they had built was no longer a partnership, it was a balancing act. A game of keeping score. And twenty years in, the debts were adding up.

*"Love doesn't hurt; it heals."*

✝

# The Smiths

The Smiths looked like any other couple: mid-thirties, two kids, a modest home in a working-class neighborhood, and matching tattoos they got during a drunken trip to Vegas. But if you stepped one foot into their world, you would realize what everyone on their street already knew: love, for James and Tonya Smith, was a battlefield, sometimes literal.

They didn't fight like most couples do. There was no silent treatment, no cold shoulders or passive aggression. Their love screamed, loud, raw, unapologetic. Yelling was foreplay. Name-calling was just Tuesday. And throwing beer bottles, lamps, or whatever was within reach? That was how they said, "I need you."

Their relationship didn't deteriorate into violence; it was built on it. The first time James told Tonya he loved her, he had a busted lip from the punch she landed after he flirted with a bartender. She laughed when he said it, blood staining his teeth. "That's how I know it's real," she would whisper, licking her knuckles.

To the Smiths, pain meant passion. Every bruise was a love note. Every arrest, a twisted badge of commitment. "If it ain't real, it don't hurt," Tonya once told a social worker who came knocking after a particularly loud altercation. That worker never came back.

Their fights were like storms: sudden, explosive, and usually ending with the two of them clinging to each other like survivors of a shipwreck. Police sirens became as familiar as the hum of their fridge. When neighbors called 911, it wasn't out of concern, it was protocol. And each time, one of them would end up in handcuffs, and the other would show up in court with a smirk and bail money.

They wore their arrests like trophies.

One time, James spent 48 hours in county jail after allegedly choking Tonya during a fight over a phone call she wouldn't explain. He was released with a restraining order, but she met him in the parking lot with her arms wide open. "You should've choked me harder," she laughed, pressing her lips to his. "Maybe next time I'll shut the hell up." And they laughed like teenagers in love, high on chaos and codependence.

Their children, silent witnesses to the war zone they called home, learned early not to ask questions. When the glass shattered or a table flipped, the kids would retreat to their room, turn up the volume on the TV, and wait for the sounds of violence to give way to the eerie calm that always followed. Sometimes the calm was worse, the kind that settled after destruction, like smoke after a fire.

Anyone who dared comment on the dysfunction found themselves united against a force stronger than logic: the Smiths' loyalty to each other. Friends tried, once. Family members intervened, once. But as soon as anyone pointed out the toxicity, Tonya and James would transform from opponents to a ruthless team, defending their love like a religion.

"You don't know what we've been through," Tonya would say, arms crossed, eyes wild. "We ride or die."

James would chime in, "People wish they had what we have. We fight hard because we love hard. If you ain't got someone willing to break something over your head, you ain't got real love."

They believed that.

To them, love was supposed to hurt. Supposed to burn. It wasn't romantic unless it left a mark. They had no blueprint for softness, no model of love that didn't involve shouting matches and midnight makeups that tasted of whiskey and tears. Their childhoods, each marked by abusive parents and unstable homes, had primed them to believe that dysfunction was the default. That love came with fists, slammed doors, and sirens.

Over time, they became legends in their neighborhood. Notorious. Everyone knew the Smiths. The cops knew their address by heart. Bartenders knew when not to serve them. Teachers at their kids' school scheduled parent conferences during school hours, when they were less likely to show up drunk or bleeding. But despite the history, the warnings, and the destruction, Tonya and James saw no problem.

This was love. Their love.

They were addicted to the highs and lows, the cycle of destruction and repair. Like addicts chasing the first high, they found themselves trapped in an endless loop of explosions and apologies. And the truth was, neither of them knew who they were without the chaos. The drama gave them identity. Made them feel alive.

On quiet days, which were rare, they would get uneasy. If things went too smoothly, if too many hours passed without an argument, someone would start a fight just to break the silence. Tonya might accuse James of cheating, or James might demand to see her phone. It didn't matter if there was truth in the accusations. What mattered was the rush, the spike of adrenaline, the confirmation that something was *happening*.

They tried therapy once. A court-ordered session after James was arrested for pushing Tonya down the stairs during an argument about unpaid bills. The therapist, a soft-spoken woman with kind eyes, asked them to describe what love meant to them. Tonya said it was "being willing to kill or die for someone." James said it was "not walking away, no matter how bad it gets."

They were both serious. The therapist made a note, paused, and gently asked if they thought love could exist without violence. They looked at each other, confused, like she had asked them to breathe underwater. After two sessions, they stopped going.

By year ten, their bodies had aged prematurely from stress, substance abuse, and violence. Tonya had a permanent scar over her left eye from a thrown bottle. James walked with a limp from a night when she rammed his leg with the car during an argument. But they still laughed. Still made love like it was war. Still told people they were "ride or die," like a badge of honor.

But underneath it all, there was weariness.

Tonya sometimes stared out the window late at night, smoking in silence. James sometimes sat on the porch alone, nursing a beer and looking at nothing. There were cracks in the armor, tiny signs that, just maybe, even they were starting to wonder if love was supposed to look like this.

One night, after a particularly brutal fight, their teenage son, who had mostly stayed silent through the years, stood in the middle of the living room and shouted, "This isn't love. It's just pain with lipstick on it."

Tonya slapped him.

Not out of malice, but reflex, because that's how she responded to confrontation. James didn't stop her. But later that night, when their son locked his door and wouldn't speak to them, they both sat in the hallway, backs against the wall, not speaking either.

For the first time, the silence wasn't waiting to be broken. It just *was*.

They didn't stop fighting after that. But the fights became less frequent. More tired. Like even the fire that had fueled their dysfunction was running out of oxygen. The yelling turned into muttering. The smashing turned into slamming doors. The arrests became fewer, replaced by long nights apart.

And in those quiet moments, the Smiths began to understand something no one had been able to convince them of before: that love without violence wasn't boring, it was healing. That peace didn't mean indifference. That, just maybe, what they called love was just fear of being alone.

It wasn't a Hollywood ending. They didn't suddenly change overnight. They still argued. Still had old habits. But they started asking questions they never had before: "What are we teaching our kids?" "Do you think we deserve better?" "Can we try something different?"

And slowly, painfully, they began to unlearn what they had always believed about love.

✝

# Rylee

Rylee was not the kind of man who didn't understand love. No, he knew exactly what it looked like. He knew its texture, its tone, its habits. He knew how it cradled a person, how it protected, how it endured. He had studied it like a thief studies a lock. Not because he wanted to give love, but because he wanted to extract it, hoard it, siphon it, control it. He didn't want to be loved for the sake of connection. He wanted to be loved like a monument is worshipped, silently, relentlessly, and without question.

He met her, Maya, in the usual way. She was soft-spoken, yet not weak. Grounded, not arrogant. Beautiful, but unaware of just how much. She was everything Rylee saw as valuable. Not because he loved her, he didn't know how, but because she was a prize. A reflection. If he could get her to love him, he would appear more worthy. She would validate him just by standing next to him.

From the beginning, Maya was all in. She offered her time, her care, her forgiveness. She assumed the best in him, even when there was little evidence to support it. Rylee noticed this early on. Most people would demand reciprocity. Most people would say, "I need you to show up for me, too." But Maya, Maya gave without keeping score.

And Rylee took without shame.

He began by testing her. Telling small lies. Saying he had called when he hadn't. Flirting openly but denying it when confronted. Watching her face for cracks. She held firm. "I trust you," she would say with a kind of naïveté that made him smirk internally. Not because he respected her faith, but because it made it easier to deceive her. Easier to conquer.

But the deeper she loved, the less he respected her.

Rylee craved something Maya didn't have, a cruelty, a distance. He didn't want love; he wanted to feel powerful in the presence of someone else's love. He needed her to need him, but he could never allow her to feel needed. He praised her only when others were listening. In private, he would downplay her achievements.

"You only got that promotion because they felt sorry for you," he would say, folding his arms with a bored look on his face. "It's not like you're really that good at what you do."

When Maya invited him to family events, he would attend, but not as a guest. He acted like a spy. He asked questions, disguised as charm, and filed away the answers like weapons. He took mental notes of her mother's anxiety, her father's silence, her brother's ambitions. He would later twist them in conversations with his own friends, mocking the very people who welcomed him into their lives.

He didn't want to be part of her world. He wanted to own it.

And yet, he would constantly remind her, "You're lucky to have me. I am the only one who understands you. Without me, you would just be floating."

That was his favorite line. He used it often. Especially after he hurt her. Especially after she cried.

Because every time she tried to leave or even imagined it, he had become who she first met again. Gentle. Loving. Apologetic. He would send flowers. Write long texts about how he realized how wrong he had been. Call her in the middle of the night just to say, "I miss the way you breathe when you sleep." Maya, believing in redemption, she always went back.

But with every return, a new piece of her stayed behind.

It wasn't just emotional exhaustion. It was something deeper. A fracturing of identity. She began to question her own worth. Her own sanity. Rylee never screamed at her. Never raised a hand. But he tore her down with surgical precision. He would point out how "clingy" she was becoming. How "insecure" she acted when she asked where he had been. When she needed reassurance, he would accuse her of being "too emotional" or "needy."

Meanwhile, Rylee lived on a diet of external validation. He needed his friends to see him as desirable. He needed women to flirt with him. He needed people to believe he was more successful, more confident, more essential than he really was. He would fabricate stories about Maya, claiming she was obsessive, unstable, even manipulative. He would read her text messages aloud to others, cherry-picking lines to frame her as desperate. All while telling her, "You're the one who needs me."

Maya tried everything. She changed her schedule to spend more time with him. She listened, compromised, apologized even when she was not wrong. She made herself smaller, more agreeable. She thought, "If I just love him harder, he'll see."

But Rylee didn't want to see. He wanted her blind.

Because as long as she could not recognize his cruelty, he could keep feeding off her light.

He attached himself to her successes, calling them "ours" but taking the credit in private. When she bought a car, he joked it was only because he told her which one to get. When she started her business, he said it was "his idea" originally. He told people, "She'd be nowhere without me," and he believed it because he needed to.

Rylee was tall only when others were on their knees.

But when Maya finally left, when she said nothing and just walked out the door, he panicked. Not because he missed her, but because he missed the feeling of being necessary. He blew up her phone. Called her mother. Showed up at her workplace with tears in his eyes. "Please," he whispered, "I have changed. I have been in therapy. I finally get it."

And Maya, predictably, painfully let him back in.

He was kind for a few days. Thoughtful. Attentive. And then, just like always, he returned to himself. His pedestal. His mask. He showed her messages from other women, not to confess, but to flaunt. He told her, "You're not the only one who wants me, you know," with a cruel sort of pride. He mocked the months she had spent healing as though they were a phase. He told her friends she begged to return. That he only took her back out of pity.

Maya watched the life drain from her own eyes one day while looking at a picture she had took beside him. Watched the hope fade. The ache turn into numbness. She no longer cried. Not because she was strong, but because she was tired. Emotionally bankrupt. She had offered every part of herself, and he had hollowed it out.

That's the thing with people like Rylee; they don't want partners. They want mirrors. They want someone to reflect back a version of themselves they can admire. They want someone to clap for their mediocrity, to validate their illusion of greatness. And the moment you stop reflecting their fantasy, you become disposable.

Rylee didn't notice the last time she left. She didn't slam a door or scream. She simply didn't come home. He texted. She didn't answer. He showed up. She wasn't there. He told their mutual friends that she was "going through something," trying to preserve the illusion that he had left her, not the other way around.

But privately, he began to unravel.

He reached out to old flames. They didn't respond. He told himself she'd come back again, she always did. But weeks passed. Then months. And slowly, he began to feel the weight of a foreign silence. There were no texts needing his attention. No arguments to win. No one to belittle. He was left alone with himself, and Rylee, without someone else's worth to siphon, was unbearably empty.

He tried to rebuild the image. Found someone new. Told the same jokes. Wore the same mask. But it never quite felt the same. Because now, he knew. He knew that someone had truly seen him and left. Not out of anger, but out of survival.

And there is no greater injury to a man like Rylee than being abandoned by someone who once loved him entirely.

Maya, on the other hand, did not become whole overnight. Healing wasn't a straight path. She still sometimes wondered if she had imagined the worst parts. She reread old messages, trying to make sense of it. But the longer she stayed away, the clearer it became:

It was never love. It was never partnership.

It was extraction.

And her freedom didn't lie in proving she was worthy of his kindness.

Her freedom was in realizing she never needed it in the first place.

*"The hollow parts of love vibrate on an unknown frequency."*

✝

*"What we call empathy is sometimes merely a gesture of support
in disguise."*

✝

# Kaylee

Kaylee always knew how to make an entrance. She could walk into a room and within minutes, all eyes were on her, whether out of admiration, curiosity, or unease. There was something magnetic about her, something in her wide, expressive eyes and the dramatic pauses she took before speaking, as though every word from her mouth were a perfectly timed line from a film. But behind that magnetic facade was a cold and calculated mind, one that thrived not on connection, but on control.

People often described Kaylee as intense. Some called her passionate, others said she was troubled. Those who got too close found themselves pulled into a whirlwind of chaos and confusion. She never had lasting friendships. At first, her charm drew people in. She could be incredibly generous, offering compliments, attention, and support that felt almost intoxicating. But once someone was within her orbit, the mask began to slip.

Kaylee lied easily. It wasn't just a defense mechanism or a way to avoid consequences, it was a sport, a form of entertainment. If someone confided in her, she would twist their secrets into a story that helped her, or worse, turn it into a weapon. She would lie to cause fights between friends, accuse people of things they never did, or play the victim to steal sympathy and attention from others.

She had an instinct for finding vulnerabilities. If someone were insecure, she would praise them in public and undermine them in private. If someone were grieving or struggling, she would swoop in with over-the-top support, only to exploit their pain later. Every interaction was a game, and the prize was control. The more someone cared, the more power she had over them, and she knew exactly when to press or pull away.

But when Kaylee was confronted, when her manipulations were uncovered or someone tried to distance themselves from her, the performance would begin.

She could cry on command. Her tears came not from regret or pain, but from a calculated awareness of how they made others feel. Her voice would shake, her body would tremble, and she would claim to be misunderstood, mistreated, broken. People, not wanting to believe someone could fake such pain, would rally around her. And once she had them back in her corner, she would use them again.

It was a cycle that repeated itself endlessly. People came and went, most walking away confused and emotionally drained, wondering if they had done something wrong. Those who confronted her left with a target on their back. Kaylee made sure that anyone who exposed her was painted as jealous, unstable, or cruel. She needed the spotlight, and if someone tried to pull it away from her, she would do anything, **anything** to get it back.

Even cruelty became a performance. If Kaylee felt ignored or overshadowed, she would stir up chaos just to bring attention back to herself. She might start a rumor, fake a crisis, or even harm someone emotionally just to regain center stage. She didn't see people as people; she saw them as props, set pieces in the drama that was her life. Empathy was a foreign language she had learned to mimic, not feel.

One time, a friend named Hannah confronted her. Hannah had caught Kaylee in a lie, Kaylee had told their mutual friends that

Hannah had cheated on her boyfriend, a complete fabrication. Kaylee's face twisted, her eyes filling with tears. She dropped to the floor, sobbing and accusing Hannah of betrayal, claiming she was being bullied. It was an Oscar-worthy performance. Within a day, Hannah was being shunned, while Kaylee basked in the glow of sympathy and social media posts filled with heart emojis and prayers.

And once the dust settled, Kaylee went right back to her games.

Her hunger for attention was insatiable. If she wasn't being talked about, she felt invisible. She had to be the center of every story, every gathering, every whispered conversation. If someone else got praise, love, or admiration, she would find a way to undercut it, subtly at first, but more aggressively if necessary. She wasn't above faking emergencies, illnesses, even threats against her life, if it meant she could be the star of the show again.

The strange thing was, Kaylee never seemed happy. She had moments of triumph, certainly, times when she manipulated people so well that even the most skeptical became her defenders. But true joy eluded her. Her relationships were shallow, built on deceit. Her victories were hollow, temporary distractions from a deeper emptiness she refused to face. She didn't want love or trust, she wanted devotion, fear, and undivided attention.

People around her began to compare stories. As her lies unraveled, more former friends began to realize they weren't alone in their experiences. The same patterns. The same betrayals. The same gaslighting. But still, confronting Kaylee remained dangerous. She was relentless in retaliation, using fake social media accounts, anonymous tips, even contacting people's families to stir up more chaos.

But eventually, her tactics started to lose their power. More people began to see through the facade. She found it harder to keep new friends, and harder still to maintain the illusion with old ones. The tears didn't work as well. The stories began to repeat. The desperation for attention became more obvious.

And when she realized she was losing her audience, she spiraled.

She staged an elaborate public breakdown posting vague threats and dramatic photos, hinting at tragedy. For a moment, the attention came rushing back, the sympathy, the concern. But this time, it didn't last. People had grown wary. Some offered support out of habit, others out of guilt, but most simply stayed away.

Kaylee was alone, truly alone, for the first time. But even then, she didn't reflect or change. She blamed others, called them cruel, ungrateful, heartless. She believed she had done nothing wrong, that people were jealous or too weak to handle her brilliance. She refused to acknowledge the wake of emotional wreckage she had left behind.

Even in solitude, Kaylee remained consumed by her need for the spotlight. She would spend hours online, creating fake accounts, writing posts that made her sound like a martyr, a survivor, a misunderstood genius. She continued weaving tales of abuse, betrayal, and rebirth, hoping to rebuild the stage where she could once again be adored.

But the world had moved on.

Kaylee was not forgotten, she was remembered by many, but not with affection. Her name became a warning, a shared lesson among those who once knew her. People grew stronger from their time with her, more aware of the red flags, more attuned to manipulation. In her quest to be unforgettable, she had become a cautionary tale.

Yet Kaylee did not see it that way. In her mind, the audience was simply asleep, and one day they would awaken and realize how wrong they had been. She waited for that moment, clinging to the fantasy of her triumphant return.

Because for Kaylee, the show could never end.

# Carlo & Elena

Carlo had always thought the world owed him something, a kind of bitter entitlement that festered behind his charming grin and carefully styled hair. To outsiders, he was magnetic: a man who could hold attention with the ease of someone born to lead. But behind his mask, that charisma took a darker form.

His wife, Elena, once dazzled by his intensity and boldness, had married him when she was twenty-three. Now, nearly a decade later, the lines of time had etched softly onto her face, and motherhood had changed the shape of her body, but not her soul, though Carlo made her feel otherwise.

He had grown crueler with age, his words sharper, his glances colder. He would eye her across the kitchen table and say things like, "You know, I could have left a long time ago. Most men would've." When she asked him what he meant, he would sigh theatrically. "You have let yourself go, Elena. You're not young anymore. I just… get bored, okay? It's not like I'm doing anything other men wouldn't."

And then he would vanish for hours, even days. When he returned, he carried the scent of other women, perfume she didn't wear, lip gloss that shimmered in the corners of his mouth, sometimes even faint bruises on his neck that mocked her in silence. She knew. He never bothered to hide it.

"You should be thankful," he once told her as they argued over dinner. "You should be on your knees thanking me for not leaving. No one else would want you now."

Each insult chipped away at something inside her. It wasn't just the betrayal of his affairs. It was the deliberate erosion of her self-worth. Carlo wasn't merely unfaithful; he was calculated in his cruelty. He reminded her constantly that he preferred younger women, that looking at her every day was like "living in the past." Sometimes, when she tried to confront him, he'd smirk and say, "What are you going to do? Leave me? Please."

The thing about constant humiliation is that it doesn't just hurt, it numbs. Elena began to feel herself floating above her life, watching a stranger absorb these blows, nod along to abuse, trying to smile through shame.

Until one evening, she defended herself.

Carlo had come home late again, reeking of gin and arrogance. He flopped onto the couch and started laughing to himself. Elena was cleaning up the living room, trying not to ask questions, trying to keep the peace. Then he looked at her and said, casually, "Met a twenty-two-year-old tonight. She actually listens when I talk. You could learn a thing or two."

She froze.

He went on. "You know, I sometimes wish you would just disappear. It's exhausting pretending I don't hate waking up next to you."

He laughed again. That laugh, it wasn't just mean, it was gleeful. As though the pain he inflicted was entertainment. Elena stood there for a long moment. Something ancient and silent moved through her. She looked down. Her hand was resting on one of her heels, sleek, sharp, innocent in appearance.

She picked it up.

There was no shouting, no warning. She didn't scream. She didn't curse. She just walked across the room and brought the heel down across his face.

Once. Then twice. Then again.

Carlo howled, blood spurting from his lip, his brow, his cheekbone. He stumbled backward, screaming her name now, pleading. But Elena was not Elena in that moment. She was every insult he ever threw. She was every night she cried in secret. She was every younger woman he paraded in front of her. She was the silence she was forced to swallow and the shame he taught her to wear.

When it was over, she dropped the heel beside him, calmly walked to the front door, and called the police herself.

Elena was arrested, charged with assault, and sentenced to a year in jail, plus 300 hours of community service. She didn't argue. She didn't weep in court. She wore her orange jumpsuit like armor and served her time quietly.

In prison, for the first time in years, no one reminded her of her age. No one sneered at her body. Other women asked her what happened, and when she told them, they nodded. Some even hugged her. For a brief, strange period of time, she was seen, not as the withered wife of a cruel man, but as someone who had finally, if violently, said "enough."

But the outside world didn't wait kindly.

When she was released, she had nowhere else to go. Her parents had long passed. Her friends had drifted, many uncomfortable with what she had done or rather, uncomfortable with the mirror it held up to their own lives. The job market was cold. Landlords even colder.

And so, one gray morning, she found herself back at the house. Their house.

Carlo opened the door with a damaged eye that hadn't fully healed and a crooked smile. "You done playing hero?"

Elena didn't respond. She walked in quietly and dropped her bag by the door. He didn't apologize. He never would. Instead, he went back to the couch and turned on the television like nothing had happened.

The house was exactly as she remembered it, suffocating, sterile, echoing with unspoken wars.

She told herself it was temporary. Just until she got back on her feet. But days turned into weeks. And weeks began to blur.

The thing about abuse, especially psychological abuse, is that it's a maze. And even when you think you have escaped, part of you still hears the echo of your name being called from its walls.

Carlo wasn't violent anymore, at least not physically. He treaded carefully now. But he didn't have to raise his voice. His silence was sharp enough. He began again with the comments, quieter now, more insidious.

"You should be grateful," he whispered one night. "Not many men would take back a woman who beat their face in with a shoe."

And for a while, she believed him.

Shame is a powerful leash. It wraps around your ankles and whispers that no one else will ever want you, that this is the best you will get, that your one act of resistance proves you're just as awful as him.

But there was one difference now.

Elena remembered what it felt like to fight back. To hurt him. To remind him, if only once, that she was not invisible. That memory pulsed inside her like a stubborn heartbeat.

She stayed, for now. But the ground beneath her was no longer solid. She began to write in a journal. To keep a secret savings account. To take long walks and sometimes, just sometimes, look strangers in the eye again.

Carlo didn't notice.

He thought he had broken her.

But there's a difference between a woman who stays because she's weak and a woman who stays because she's gathering her strength.

Elena had been through the fire. She had struck the match. She had paid the price.

And somewhere deep inside her, she knew: the next time she left, it wouldn't be with a weapon.

It would be with peace.

And she wouldn't come back.

✝

*"Echoes from childhood can shape an entire reality."*

# Ava

From the moment she could understand the world, Ava was taught that love had to be earned. Her father, a man who demanded admiration and obedience, loomed large in every room he entered. To the outside world, he was charming, successful, even charismatic. But to the inside world, he was unpredictable, controlling, and coldly dismissive. He praised Ava only when she served his needs, when she was quiet, agreeable, and made him look good. Any attempts to assert herself were met with mockery or cold silence. Love, in her young mind, became associated with performance, fear, and the desperate chase for approval.

As Ava grew older, she carried her father's voice inside her like a second conscience. It criticized her when she showed vulnerability, berated her when she craved comfort, and shamed her for wanting to be seen. Her nervous system, finely tuned to the emotional weather of abuse, had been shaped by survival. She knew how to anticipate emotional withdrawal, how to make herself small, and how to find value only in others' validation. This was what love felt like to her: uneasy, consuming, and always just out of reach.

In her teenage years and early twenties, Ava unconsciously gravitated toward men who reminded her of her father. Men who were self-absorbed, dismissive, and emotionally unavailable. She mistook their aloofness for strength. Their indifference felt familiar. Their attention when she could manage to earn it, felt like the most intoxicating kind of love. When one of these men would compliment her or show brief affection, it triggered a rush of dopamine the same rare high she once felt as a little girl when her father would finally offer a crumb of praise.

Again, Ava entered relationships where she felt the need to prove her worth. She tolerated emotional neglect, manipulation, and even cruelty, telling herself this was passion, that love was supposed to hurt a little. When these relationships inevitably became toxic or fell apart, she felt devastated but strangely validated. Heartbreak, after all, was proof that she had cared deeply. And caring deeply, she believed, was a kind of virtue.

But something began to shift when Ava met Daniel.

Daniel was unlike anyone she had dated before. He was gentle, honest, emotionally present. He listened when she spoke, remembered intricate details, and genuinely seemed to care about her wellbeing. At first, Ava was intrigued. Part of her longed for this kind of tenderness, a part of her had been starved of safety stirred to life. But as their relationship unfolded, discomfort set in.

Daniel's kindness felt suspicious. It felt wrong.

He would text her good morning and ask about her day, and she would roll her eyes. When he expressed his feelings with vulnerability, she felt embarrassed for him. "Why are you being so soft?" she would snap one evening when he opened up about a rough week at work. "Real men don't complain."

Ava started testing him. She canceled plans last minute, flirted with other men in front of him, criticized his hobbies. She pushed his boundaries, waiting for the anger, the emotional retreat, the abandonment. She needed him to prove that he could hurt her because hurt, to her, meant love. His unwavering calmness infuriated her. Instead of fighting back, he tried to understand her behavior. Instead of withdrawing, he stayed steady.

She accused him of being weak. "You let people walk all over you," she said. "You are a coward. No spine."

He didn't lash out, but he didn't stay indefinitely either. Eventually, he set a boundary of his own and walked away, not with drama or cruelty, but with sadness and clarity.

The night he left, Ava sat alone in her apartment, flooded with guilt and confusion. She had driven away the one person who had tried to love her in a healthy way, and she didn't know why. The grief came in waves, first as anger, then as shame, then as a deep hollow sadness she couldn't explain. This pattern had repeated so many times, and she didn't know how to stop it.

Her heart mourned his absence. The safety he brought had started to feel right, even if her mind rejected it. But that safety also felt boring, unfamiliar, too exposed. Vulnerability had always equaled danger. It meant being judged, dismissed, or left. It was safer to sabotage the good than to be caught off guard by its loss.

She began talking to friends and wanted their honest opinion on how they saw her.

For the first time, Ava traced the lines from her childhood to her adult relationships. She learned how children of narcissistic parents often grow up believing that love is conditional, that they must shrink, twist, or betray themselves to be worthy. She understood how her father's emotional neglect had rewired her brain to associate love with anxiety, pursuit, and instability. The concept of being loved simply for existing felt odd to her. She had never been taught that it was even possible.

Through therapy, Ava started to see Daniel's behavior in a new light. His gentleness wasn't weakness; it was strength. The fact that he didn't retaliate, that he set boundaries and chose peace, those were signs of emotional maturity, not cowardice. She began to recognize the deep fear she carried, the fear that if someone truly saw her, they would leave. So, she pushed people away first. Better to hurt them than risk being hurt herself.

It took time, years even, for Ava to untangle the wires. Her body still sometimes flinched when someone got too close emotionally. She still found herself drawn, on occasion, to the thrill of aloof men who reminded her of the past. But she no longer acted on those impulses blindly. She could pause now, reflect, choose differently.

She began surrounding herself with people who mirrored Daniel's energy, friends who she never saw were kind, present, and emotionally intelligent. Slowly, she rewired her definition of love.

It wasn't a chase.

It wasn't a battle.

It wasn't earned by suffering.

Love was consistent. It was gentle. It was being known and still chosen.

Ava wrote a letter to Daniel that she never sent. In it, she apologized for the ways she had projected her pain onto him. She thanked him for showing her what real love could look like, even if she hadn't been ready for it at the time.

"I used to think kindness was weakness," she wrote. "Now I see it as the greatest strength. You were brave in ways I didn't understand, because I was still at war with myself."

Years later, when she did meet someone new, someone with Daniel's heart and his own unique light, Ava didn't flinch the way she used to. She still was afraid, but she met it with compassion instead of sabotage. She let herself be loved, and more importantly, she began learning to love herself without conditions.

The ghosts of her childhood had not vanished, but they no longer steered the wheel. Ava had reclaimed the pen from her past and begun writing a new story, one, not not based on pain, but on healing. On choice. On a love that was not earned but received.

And in that love, she finally found who Ava was.

$$\dagger$$

*"When in Rome, we don't always do what the Romans do; we're just visiting."*

✝

*"God hates the utterance of bad speech except by those who have been wronged."*

✝

# Ly

It started with a wrong number.

Ly was not trying to meet anyone new that day. She was simply trying to reach a friend. The call went through, but the voice on the other end wasn't the one she expected.

"Sorry, I think you have the wrong number," the man said. His tone was kind, and there was something warm about his voice, something familiar, like a song she had once loved but forgotten.

"Oh, I'm sorry," she said, ready to hang up.

"Wait," he interrupted. "You have a beautiful voice. I, I know this is random, but I have been feeling alone lately."

Ly paused. The man sounded sincere, almost sad. As odd as the situation was, she didn't feel creeped out or threatened. Just... curious.

The man, let us call him Marco, had just come off a terrible argument with his longtime girlfriend. Their relationship had been rocky for months, and that night, he had been drinking alone, scrolling through his thoughts, and wondering what he was even doing with his life.

Talking to Ly was like to open a window in a stuffy room. She was witty, warm, and real. Their first conversation lasted only a few minutes, but it left an impression on both of them.

The next day, he called her.

That call lasted two hours.

They talked about everything, childhood memories, music they liked, places they wanted to travel. There was an instant comfort between them, like two people who had met long ago and were now just remembering.

Within a week, they decided to meet in person. They chose a beach concert on a warm Saturday night. The music pulsed through the sand, and the sky was lit with stars and stage lights. When their eyes met for the first time, it felt surreal. He smiled. She smiled. And just like that, they were pulled into each other's orbit.

The following weeks were intense. Marco was everything Ly had thought she wanted, romantic, spontaneous, full of affection. He would send flowers to her work, write her long messages at night, and talk endlessly about their future together. She knew he still had a girlfriend, but he insisted it was over emotionally, and he was only staying out of obligation until he figured out a way to leave without hurting anyone.

Six months in, he finally ended things with his girlfriend. It was messy, but he told Ly it was worth it. A year after their first phone call, Marco and Ly got married in a small but heartfelt ceremony.

Ly became pregnant almost immediately. They were both overjoyed, and their home filled with baby clothes, paint swatches for the nursery, and dreams of family picnics and bedtime stories.

Their first son was born healthy and radiant, filling their home with laughter and sleepless nights.

But life, as it often does, had its own plans.

Two years into their marriage, Ly suffered from an ectopic pregnancy. The pain was sharp, both physically and emotionally. It was a terrifying ordeal, one that left scars far deeper than medical charts could ever reflect.

Still, she held on to hope. Six months later, she became pregnant again. This time, everything went smoothly, and she gave birth to their second son, a moment she describes as both terrifying and beautiful, given all they had been through.

But something had shifted in Marco.

After their second child was born, he began to grow distant. He no longer came home with the same smile. The long conversations turned into monosyllabic replies. He stopped planning date nights, skipped family events, and seemed to live more in his phone than in their home.

Ly tried to reach him, to pull him back into the life they had built. But every attempt was met with either distraction or silence.

Then the truth emerged.

Marco had been unfaithful. Not just once, not just casually, but deeply, and painfully so. He had gotten his friend's niece pregnant. The woman was already a mother, and their affair had not been a momentary lapse in judgment but an ongoing betrayal.

When Ly confronted him, the explanation he offered felt more like manipulation than remorse.

"She's like family," he argued. "She has no place to go. I think it would be the right thing to do, to let her stay here for a while. For the baby. For the kids."

Ly was stunned. Not only had he betrayed her, but now he was trying to integrate the fallout of that betrayal into their home, under the pretense of charity and familiarity duty. The insult added weight to the injury, leaving her in a place she never thought she would be questioning everything about the man she once believed was her soulmate.

Still, she tried, for the sake of their children, for the love she still carried somewhere deep within her. But the distance between them only grew wider. Marco had checked out emotionally. He became colder, less present. There were no more I-love-you, no more effort to fix what was broken.

Eventually, it became clear that she was in it alone.

What started as a storybook meeting, a chance encounter built on a wrong number and serendipity, had unraveled into a difficult, isolating reality. Love had once brought them together so powerfully, but now it felt like the only one fighting to preserve it was her.

And yet, she stood strong. She wasn't the same woman who had made that mistaken call years ago. She was now a mother of two, someone who had faced heartbreak, loss, betrayal, and the unimaginable pain of being pushed aside, but who continued to rise anyway.

She began to rebuild herself, piece by piece. Not for Marco. Not for anyone else. But for her sons, and for the version of herself who still believed in brighter days.

There is no simple ending to a story like Ly's, she didn't walk away unscathed. But she walked away wiser, and with her dignity intact.

What once began with a voice on the phone, a man who said he was lonely and captivated by her voice, ended with silence and deceit.

But in between those chapters, there was real love, real joy, and lessons that would shape her forever.

Ly now tells her story with clarity. Love, she says, can be beautiful, wild, and consuming, but it should never cost you your self-worth. And when someone shows you who they really are, believe them.

Especially if they try to disguise betrayal as love.

# Ivy

They looked like any ordinary couple, smiling in photos, taking vacations, showing up at gatherings arm-in-arm. But anyone who got close enough to her could see the cracks, the strain in her voice when she talked about him, the way her eyes darted when asked how things were going.

He had a way of turning every moment into chaos. For years, he brought more problems into her life than peace. Whenever there was something important to her, a birthday, a graduation, a family dinner, he found a way to ruin it. He didn't like sharing the spotlight, didn't like attention that wasn't focused solely on him. She started to notice a pattern: when her family was around, he would disappear. It became a joke among relatives, "Where's he hiding now?", but for her, it wasn't funny. It was exhausting.

Her family had welcomed him. They didn't have to, but they did. From the first time they met him, they had been open, warm, and supportive. They gave him a seat at the table, extended kindness he hadn't earned, and they were patient every time he acted like he didn't want to be there.

He wanted her to revolve around him, always. If he was tired, she needed to care. If he was angry, she had to soothe him. If she was busy, she had to drop everything. His moods became her responsibility, and her needs, her joy, were always second.

But she tried. God, she tried. She thought maybe love meant carrying someone until they figured out how to stand. She told herself he would change, that all he needed was more support, more care, more understanding. But no matter how much she gave, it was never enough. He took, and took, and took, until there was nothing left of her but fragments.

The cruise had been meant to be a celebration. It was his birthday, and her family, once again, included him, planned around him, paid for him, treated him like one of their own. They dressed up for dinners, posed for pictures, raised their glasses in his honor. She thought, just maybe, this time he would meet them halfway. Maybe he would finally rise to the moment.

But trouble always followed him like a fly to shh...

On the third night of the cruise, her family decided to walk the upper deck after dinner. It was one of those magical evenings, music playing softly from the outdoor speakers, the ocean stretching endlessly on all sides, stars just beginning to prick through the dusk.

But when she turned to look for him, he was gone.

At first, she thought he had gone to the restroom. Then, he was just grabbing a drink or needed a moment alone. But minutes passed. Then fifteen. Then thirty. She circled the deck, peered into lounges, called his phone, texted. Nothing.

Her family started asking, "Where'd he go?" And she didn't have an answer.

Panic mixed with shame as she searched. She went back to their cabin. Not there. Then to the bars, the casino, back to the deck. Back to the cabin. Still nothing. Her heart pounded, not because she feared for his safety, but because this was just like him. Disappearing. Making her worry. Making her explain. Making her feel like a fool.

Finally, after nearly an hour, she found him. Back in the cabin, casually lying on the bed.

"You walked off," he said coldly.

She blinked. "What?"

"You just left me."

Her stomach turned. "Are you serious? I have been looking everywhere for you. I thought something happened!"

He shrugged. "Don't make this about you."

She stared at him, stunned. "You embarrassed me in front of my family. Again."

And then, as if the moment needed more fire, he looked her dead in the eyes and said, "F*** you and your family."

The words hit her like a truck. The man she had defended repeatedly, the one her family had tried to embrace, had just spit in their face. And she snapped.

They had both been drinking, and that lowered the guardrails. Her restraint, already worn thin, just collapsed. But before she knew what she was doing, her fist connected with his mouth.

She didn't even remember thinking about it. Her body moved on its own. Rage had overtaken reason, and all the years of bottled-up frustration, humiliation, and pain came pouring out. She jumped on him, grabbing at his neck, punching him over and over again.

She could hear herself yelling, could feel her hands trembling, her heart racing. But the worst part, the part that would haunt her later, was that for a split second, it felt good. To stop being quiet. To stop swallowing the hurt. To finally show him what he had done to her.

And then it was over.

She sat on the floor, gasping for breath, hands shaking, her whole body buzzing with adrenaline and shame. He sat stunned, wiping blood from his lip, stunned silent for once.

She didn't cry right away. It was more of a numbness, a hollow silence that followed. She was horrified, not just at him, but at herself. She wasn't that person. She had never been violent before. She always believed in walking away. In being the bigger person.

But this, this was what he had done to her. This is what years of emotional manipulation, gaslighting, and cruelty had built. He had made her feel small, crazy, invisible. And she hated that she had let him bring her to this point.

She cleaned up in silence, her mind racing through everything that had led to that night. All the broken promises. The passive-aggressive comments. The way he would always twist things until she was the one apologizing, the one fixing, the one bending.

That night, as the ship rocked gently on the sea, she stared out the window, trying to figure out how she had gotten here, how she had become someone who could be pushed this far.

It wasn't about the cruise, or even the fight. It was about all the moments she had ignored, all the red flags she had explained away, all the pieces of herself she had handed over hoping he would finally value them.

He was trouble for her. From the beginning, her soul had known it. But her heart had wanted to believe otherwise.

The next morning, she didn't speak to him. She barely looked at him. Her family sensed something had happened, but no one said a word. She spent the rest of the trip in quiet reflection, slowly peeling back the layers of the life she had been living.

She knew what she had to do. The woman who stood on that cruise ship balcony was not the same woman who had fallen in love with him. That woman was gone, replaced by someone older, sadder, and finally, finally done.

She wasn't proud of the way things unfolded. But in that explosive, awful moment, she had found clarity.

Love should never cost you your dignity. It should never isolate you, manipulate you, or drive you to madness. She had made mistakes but loving him wasn't one of them, believing he would change was.

When the ship docked and they went their separate ways, she carried her bags and her guilt off that boat. But she also carried something else called freedom.

✝

# Cole

He hadn't planned on staying. When they first met, she was a whirlwind of need, beautiful, fragile, constantly in crisis. He could see it from the beginning, the way she latched on, not just to him but to anything that offered the illusion of stability. And he, with his calm presence and steady nature, became her anchor before he even knew it.

At first, it was flattering. She needed him. She called him in tears when the coffee machine broke down. She clung to him when her car wouldn't start, when her mother forgot her birthday, when her anxiety spiraled late at night. Her dependency became the glue that held them together, even as it drained him.

She couldn't keep a job for long. Couldn't handle the pressure, the structure, or the smallest of criticisms. She would call him sobbing from bathroom stalls, whispering about how unfair her boss was, how her coworkers didn't understand her. Every time, he would talk her down, remind her to breathe, then leave work early to take her home.

There was something tragic about her that pulled him in. She reminded him of a bird with a broken wing, delicate and panicked, always on the verge of collapse. And yet, she was beautiful. Not in a polished, magazine-cover way, but in a raw, unfiltered sense. Her eyes, large and doe-like, always seemed to be searching for safety. Her voice was soft, uncertain, but it carried a vulnerability that made people lean in.

He was attracted to her. That much was true. But attraction alone doesn't sustain a relationship. What kept him there, long after the excitement faded, was something else guilt, perhaps. A sense of responsibility. A belief that if he left, she might fall apart completely, and he didn't want that on his conscience.

She wasn't lazy, just lost. The world overwhelmed her. Making a phone call could take hours of mental preparation. Paying bills made her stomach hurt. Social interactions exhausted her for days. She didn't know how to cope with the basics of adulthood, and somewhere along the line, he had become her crutch.

At times, he resented it.

He had come home after a long day, looking for quiet, and find her curled up on the couch, crying over something small. The dishes would be piled up in the sink, laundry untouched, her face red from anxiety. He wanted to scream, to tell her to pull herself together. But instead, he swallowed his frustration and held her until she calmed down.

Every now and then, she would try. She would wake up early and make him breakfast or surprise him with a clean apartment. On those days, he would see a flicker of hope, that, she was getting better. But the flicker never lasted. She would slip back into her pattern, and the cycle would repeat.

He told himself he stayed because he loved her, and he did, in his own way. But more than love, it was a sense of duty. A fear of what might happen if he left. He had once found her sitting on the bathroom floor with a bottle of sleeping pills in her hand, not open, not consumed, but close enough. He had taken them away, held her for hours, and promised never to leave.

That promise haunted him.

There were good days, of course. Days when she laughed easily, when they danced in the kitchen, when she showed glimpses of strength. On those days, he felt like they had a chance. He remembered why he was drawn to her in the first place, the fire behind the fragility, the potential hidden beneath all that fear.

But those days were rare.

He began to lose parts of himself. Friends faded away, he no longer had the energy to meet them. His hobbies disappeared. His smile became something he wore like a uniform, not a feeling he actually felt. He became a caretaker more than a partner, a therapist more than a lover.

Still, he stayed.

People asked why. His parents, his coworkers, even strangers who caught a glimpse of their dynamic. But he never had an answer that made sense. How do you explain that sometimes love looks like sacrifice? That sometimes, the line between compassion and codependence blurs so much that you can't tell the difference anymore.

He wasn't a hero. He wasn't noble. He was just there and tired.

There were moments when he fantasized about leaving, about packing a bag and walking away without looking back. He imagined a quiet life, one where he didn't have to constantly reassure someone, where he didn't have to feel responsible for another person's entire emotional world.

But then he would look at her.

She would be asleep on the couch, face peaceful for once, and he would remember the girl he met at that park years ago, the girl who spoke softly but laughed hard, who had dreams before fear stole them away. He didn't know how to abandon her. He didn't know how to say, *you're too much* without it sounding like a betrayal.

So, he stayed.

Not because it was easy. Not because it was right. But because sometimes, the heart chooses comfort over freedom. Sometimes, pity disguises itself as love. And sometimes, the fear of breaking someone else keeps you collecting pieces of your own.

# Wayne

There was once a man who loved deeply and sincerely, a man whose heart was open like a door that never locked. He believed in healing through connection, in love as a sacred act. He had always longed for a partnership rooted in reciprocity, emotional safety, and truth. But despite his pure intentions, life sent him recurring lesson wrapped in different faces: women who were lost, hurting, and broken in ways they didn't always acknowledge, and certainly not in ways they intended to heal from.

They came to him not with affection, but with need. They wore sorrow like a second skin and mistook his light for the cure to their darkness. And he, the eternal empath, took them in, every time. He saw their sadness not as a flag but as a signal flare calling for help. He answered the call, always. Not because he was foolish, but because he genuinely believed in people's ability to change. He believed love could be transformative. That if someone felt truly seen, perhaps they could begin to see themselves too.

He was kind. Not in a performative or transactional way, but in the way that made people feel safe in their silence. He listened more than he spoke. He offered comfort where others had imposed conditions. And for a while, each of these women felt like maybe, just maybe this man was the one who would save them. But what they didn't realize, or refused to admit, was that healing never comes from outside of oneself. And so, instead of rising with him, they leaned.

They leaned too hard.

What began as affection turned into dependence. Conversations about dreams and shared futures were slowly replaced by constant emotional rescue missions. His life began to revolve around soothing storms he didn't create. He became a sponge, soaking up every drop of their unprocessed grief. And in doing so, he started to disappear.

Piece by piece, he gave himself away. First his time, then his energy. Then his joy. Until one day, he didn't recognize the man that he was. The vibrant, creative, and passionate soul who once moved through the world with ease and lightness now carried the weight of other people's wounds like a second spine. He had become a home for everyone but himself.

And yet, he stayed.

Not because he didn't know better, but because he didn't want to give up on anyone. He had grown up believing that love meant staying. That you didn't walk away from people when they were at their lowest. That leaving meant you had failed. But no one ever taught him that sometimes, love means letting go. That staying in the fire to save someone else could also mean burning yourself alive.

Each relationship followed the same arc: initial intensity, followed by slow erosion. Women who had once looked at him with wonder would start to resent the very light they had been drawn to. As they failed to fill their own wells, they blamed him for their thirst. They mistook his compassion for control, his attentiveness for obligation. They took his presence for granted, until he became invisible.

And when they finally left or forced him to, they took pieces of him with them. Not physical things, but something deeper. The unspoken parts of him that he had hoped would be seen and cherished. His softness. His hope. His trust.

Still, he kept going. He didn't allow bitterness to consume him, though he had every right to let it. He still believed that the right person wouldn't see his empathy as an opportunity to take, but as a sacred space to meet him in. He still believed that love could be mutual, not a mission.

But he began to change.

He became quieter. More careful. Less willing to share the full weight of his heart. He smiled, but it didn't always reach his eyes. He gave, but not as freely. There were still flashes of the man he had always been, the man with hands ready to hold, with arms wide open but now, there was also hesitation. Caution. A quiet ache.

Sometimes at night, he would lie awake wondering if something was wrong with him. After all, he was the common denominator in every situation. But deep down, he knew it wasn't that he was broken. It was that he had never met as an equal. He had become a reflection for women who couldn't bear to see themselves clearly. And instead of asking why they didn't love their own reflection, he had tried to make the mirror more beautiful.

The truth was, he had a healer's heart, and that is both a gift and a curse in a world where many are bleeding, but few want to truly heal. He realized, eventually, that his energy wasn't limitless. That being a sanctuary for others required him to build one for himself first. That empathy without boundaries is self-destruction dressed up as virtue.

And so, slowly, he began to reclaim himself.

He stopped answering calls that only came in times of crisis. He started asking, *"Who takes care of me?"* He began seeking relationships where love was not built on rescue but on respect. Where he didn't have to earn connection through sacrifice. Where joy wasn't a reward for suffering.

He learned to let go without guilt. To love without losing himself. To recognize that someone else's sadness was not his to fix. He learned that his shine was his own not a lightbulb for others to feed off, but a sun that deserved to be nurtured, protected, and reflected.

He still loved deeply. That would never change. But now he loved wisely, too. He stopped mistaking emotional labor for intimacy. Stopped thinking that absorbing someone's pain was the same as being close to them. And when the next woman came along, sad and searching, he didn't offer to save her. He offered her honesty. Boundaries. Support, but not self-erasure.

He waited for someone who could see him, not just their own reflection in him.

And when she came, because one day, she didn't ask for his light. She brought her own.

Together, they didn't complete each other. They *complemented* each other. Two whole people, still learning, still growing, but not bleeding on each other to feel alive. They created a space where both could flourish. A partnership, not a project.

And in that, he finally found what he had been looking for all along: not just love, but peace.

✝

Talking to someone can be a powerful part of the healing process.

When you open and share the thoughts and emotions you have been holding inside, you are giving yourself permission to release the weight you have been carrying. Bottled-up feelings can become overwhelming, but speaking them aloud, especially to someone who listens without judgment, can bring clarity, relief, and a sense of connection. Sometimes, just putting your experiences into words can help you understand them better and begin to heal. You don't have to go through everything alone; talking can be the first step toward feeling lighter and more at peace.

# Ki

There was once a man who craved the thrill of being desired. He didn't want to do the chasing; he wanted to be chased. And when he met her, someone warm-hearted and full of quiet strength, he saw an opportunity.

She liked him, genuinely. But she wasn't used to being forward with men. Still, something about him pulled her in. So, she left gentle signs: a smile that lingered too long, messages that hinted at wanting more, small acts of care that said, *"I'm here if you want to meet me halfway."*

But he didn't meet her halfway. Instead, he leaned back, testing how far she would go. Each time she gave more, more vulnerability, more attention, more effort, he gave less. He mistook her affection as permission to withdraw, believing it would make her try harder. And for a while, she did.

But with each unanswered gesture and every emotional silence, something in her started to ache. It wasn't just disappointment; it was the realization that her tenderness was being used as leverage.

She wasn't angry at love. She wasn't even angry at him, not really. But she was deeply sad. Sad for putting herself out there in ways that cost her parts of her pride. Sad for hoping he would see her and want to meet her in that brave middle space between wanting and being wanted.

Worse, she began to notice similarities in the men she crossed paths with seemed to want to be adored, pursued, and flattered. They wanted to be put on a pedestal, bathed in effort and romance. And somehow, they expected her to play the role of prince charming in every story.

But she was tired. Tired of being the only one to fight for connection. Tired of dimming her own needs just to be enough for men who didn't want to match her efforts.

So, she stepped away wiser. She decided she would rather be alone than shrink herself to win someone who only wanted to be chased, not loved.

And somewhere that followed, she healed, not by chasing anyone else, but by following her heart to a place she had not known.

*"The way you speak to yourself sets the tone. Be kind, be patient, be proud."*

†

*"Lead with intent. Do the work on your own and trust the process."*

†

## "To the Soul That Stayed"

Forgive yourself for the roads not taken,
the words you choked, the hearts mistaken.
You are not the echo of every wrong,
you are the silence that learned to be strong.
Regret is a shadow that longs to stay,
but even shadows fade with the day.
Let it go. Let it pass.
You are not meant to live in the past.
The guilt you carry like a stone,
was never meant to be your own.
It taught you, yes, but lessons end, and your wounds are not the same
as sins, my dear friend.
Breathe in now.
This breath is yours, unearned yet given.
You don't need to earn permission
to be forgiven.
Stand in your truth, soft and whole.
You are not broken, only bold.
Every scar has made you real, and that is something time can't steal.
So walk on, lighter than before,
you owe the past no penance more.
Let your soul unclench, and be,
forgiveness, love, and finally… free.

*"May they leave you in peace, to all those who took your last and
hid behind their dirty little mask."*

✝

# Narcissistic Friendships: A Story of Manipulation, Envy, and Emotional Exploitation

Friendship, in its truest form, is meant to be a safe haven, a space where trust, mutual respect, and emotional reciprocity thrive. However, not all friendships live up to this ideal. Some are rooted not in love, but in manipulation, power, and control. Narcissistic friendships fall into this category, often marked by subtle abuse, jealousy, and a constant undermining of one party's worth. One of the most insidious forms of this dynamic can be found in friendships where one person wears the mask of care and camaraderie, all while working behind the scenes to sabotage the very person they claim to cherish.

In the case we explore here, the victim finds herself entangled with a so-called friend who thrives on deceit, envy, and emotional exploitation. The relationship is anything but mutual, it is one-sided, draining, and toxic at its core.

## The Green-Eyed Monster: Envy Masquerading as Friendship

Envy is often at the heart of narcissistic friendships. In this scenario, the narcissistic friend invites her own girlfriend to social gatherings, not out of inclusion or camaraderie, but as a calculated move to assert dominance. The girlfriend, confident, perhaps attractive, maybe successful, triggers something deep within her: a relentless comparison game. Rather than confronting these feelings maturely, she lashes out covertly, making fun of her in group settings, laughing at her expense, and creating an unspoken narrative that isolates her target.

This pattern of social humiliation serves a dual purpose. It elevates the narcissist in the eyes of others, making her appear as the ringleader or the "funny one," while simultaneously diminishing the self-esteem of her friend. It's not about jokes or bonding, it's about dominance, control, and feeding the ego.

## The Private Parasite: Emotional and Financial Drain

What makes narcissistic friendships even more painful is their private nature, what happens behind closed doors is often starkly different from public displays. In private, the narcissistic friend leans on her target, confiding in her, venting endlessly about her toxic relationships, seeking comfort, support, and even financial assistance.

She asks for money, not because she has no other options, but because she wants to keep her friend in a state of guilt and responsibility. She monopolizes her time, constantly burdening her with her problems, but offers nothing in return. Emotional support becomes a one-way street, and any attempt to set boundaries is met with more manipulation, guilt-tripping, or outright gaslighting.

This draining dynamic isn't an accident, it's intentional. The narcissist doesn't just need help; she craves the control that comes from making someone else feel responsible for her life, her pain, and her mistakes. At the core, she *hates* the fact that her friend is in a position to help, whether financially stable, emotionally strong, or simply independent. That hatred becomes fuel for deeper sabotage.

## Sabotage and Smear Campaigns

Perhaps the most painful part of this toxic friendship is the active effort to destroy the friend's reputation. Out of the spotlight, the narcissistic friend spreads lies, painting her as untrustworthy, selfish, or worse. These lies are designed to fracture her relationships with others, to isolate her, and to ensure that no one else sees her light.

This is a textbook example of a **smear campaign**, a tactic often used by narcissists to maintain control over their victim's social reality. By twisting facts or outright fabricating stories, the narcissist ensures that her friend's social standing is always under threat. This prevents the victim from gaining the validation or support that might empower her to walk away.

It's a cruel double life: being leaned on in private but stabbed in the back in public.

## Sexual Manipulation and Insecurity

Adding a deeper layer of toxicity is the sexual manipulation present in the relationship. The narcissist, knowing full well that her friend is in a relationship, wears revealing outfits around her man, not out of comfort or personal expression, but as a deliberate move to test boundaries and assert dominance. She wants to catch him looking, to see if she can incite jealousy or tension. When he doesn't take the bait, she retaliates, not against him, but against her friend, claiming he must be gay, that he doesn't want a woman, that something must be wrong with *her.*

This tactic is cruel, calculated, and deeply damaging. It's not just about sexual competition, it's about humiliation. It's about making her friend question her desirability, her relationship, and her sense of reality.

## Destruction of Property: The Physical Manifestation of Hate

If emotional sabotage and character assassination were not enough, the narcissistic friend takes it a step further, by physically destroying her friend's belongings. She steals, breaks, or throws away things when visiting her house. Whether it's a new piece of clothing, a gift, or anything that represents joy or success, it becomes a target for destruction.

This is more than pettiness, it is a manifestation of deep-seated resentment. Anything that symbolizes growth, happiness, or independence is a threat to the narcissist. Instead of celebrating her friend's accomplishments or joys, she looks to destroy them, because in her mind, if her friend is suffering or losing, then she is winning.

## Isolation and Withholding Celebration

Another hallmark of narcissistic friendships is emotional withholding. Whenever something good happens in the friend's life, whether it's a new job, a new relationship, or a personal achievement, the narcissist pulls away. Instead of celebrating, she minimizes it, finds flaws, or ignores it altogether.

This absence is a form of punishment. It's the narcissist's way of saying, "You are not allowed to outshine me." If she cannot be the center of attention, she would rather see the whole moment ruined.

## The Psychology Behind the Behavior

At the core of narcissistic abuse is deep insecurity. The narcissist views others not as people, but as tools, props in the theater of her own life. Anyone who challenges her perceived superiority becomes a threat, even if they are a friend. Particularly in this case, the narcissist is likely battling unresolved envy, abandonment wounds, and a desperate need for external validation. Rather than address these internal issues, she externalizes them, projecting hatred and blame onto someone who poses no harm, only support.

But this is also what makes it so toxic. The friend is not an enemy, she's someone who tries to help, who listens, who gives, who shows up. That is what makes the betrayal even more painful.

## Healing and Moving On

Escaping a narcissistic friendship is no easy feat. Victims are often left with broken trust, shattered self-esteem, and a lingering sense of confusion: *Was it all in my head? Did I do something wrong?*

The first step toward healing is *recognition*. Acknowledging that this was not a healthy friendship, that the love was conditional and manipulative, is crucial. It's also important to understand that **you were not the problem**, your light simply exposed someone else's darkness.

Setting boundaries becomes essential. That means cutting off contact, refusing to engage in guilt-driven conversations, and choosing peace over proximity. It also means surrounding yourself with people who celebrate you, not compete with you. People who offer mutual care, not silent resentment.

Therapy, journaling, and self-reflection can aid the healing process. Many victims of narcissistic abuse benefit from learning about narcissism in depth to understand the patterns and avoid repeating them in future relationships.

## Never dim your light.

Narcissistic friendships are some of the most damaging relationships a person can experience. They often masquerade as deep bonds but are rooted in envy, control, and manipulation. In the case described, the narcissist wove a web of deceit, using her friend as an emotional crutch, financial resource, and scapegoat, all while plotting against her success and happiness.

But in every story of emotional abuse, there lies a turning point, a moment of clarity when the fog fades and the truth becomes visible. It is in this moment that the victim reclaims her life, her voice, and her right to peace. No one deserves to be hated for their light, stolen from for their success, or used for their kindness.

Walking away from a narcissistic friend may feel like loss, but in truth, it is liberation. It is the beginning of a life where joy is not punished, help is not weaponized, and love is not conditional.

# Lin

Lin had always put her daughter first. From the moment she held her newborn in her arms, she promised to protect her no matter what. Through long nights, scraped knees, heartbreaks, and graduations, Lin had been there, quietly strong, always present. But now, years later, that unwavering bond between mother and daughter was being tested in ways Lin never imagined possible. The person responsible wasn't a stranger or a distant relative, but someone Lin had invited into their lives: her boyfriend.

He moved in just after her daughter left for college. At first, he seemed charming, attentive, even helpful. Lin had been lonely for a long time. Her daughter, now a young adult, was off pursuing her own life, and Lin believed she was finally allowed to have her own. Someone to share meals with. Someone to lean on. But gradually, his charm peeled away, revealing something odd.

It started subtly. When Lin would get off the phone with her daughter, he would make dismissive comments.

"She's still calling you that much? She's in college, Lin. She doesn't need her mommy anymore."

Lin would chuckle awkwardly, unsure how to respond. Was he joking? Trying to be light-hearted? But the remarks didn't stop. They grew more frequently, more pointed.

"She's manipulating you," he said one evening while Lin scrolled through text messages from her daughter. "She's using guilt to keep you wrapped around her finger. You need to let go."

Lin frowned. That didn't sound like her daughter at all. She was strong, independent, and always tried to be considerate of Lin's feelings. But she didn't say anything. She didn't want to start a fight.

Soon, it escalated. When Lin's daughter came home for a weekend visit, things felt off. The boyfriend was cold, distant. He barely acknowledged her, and when he did, it was with clipped tones or passive-aggressive remarks. Lin tried to smooth things over, urging her daughter to be patient.

"He's just not used to having other people in the house," Lin whispered in the kitchen as her daughter stood stiffly beside her. "Give him time."

But time didn't help. In fact, things only got worse when her daughter left.

"He's a bad influence on you," he told Lin the next day. "She thinks she knows better than everyone. She's disrespectful. Arrogant. A brat, if we're being honest."

Lin's heart sank. Those were harsh words, and they didn't align with the daughter she knew. Yes, they had their disagreements, like any mother and daughter, but to call her a brat? It felt cruel. Still, she didn't challenge him. She simply turned away, pretending she hadn't heard.

And then came the accusations. Every time Lin's daughter disagreed with something, about the way her mother was treated, or how little she was called or visited, he twisted it into something sinister.

"She's trying to turn you against me," he said one evening after Lin hung up the phone. "She's toxic, Lin. She makes you feel guilty for being happy. That's not love. That's control."

Lin didn't know what to say. She had started to feel torn between the two people she loved most. Her boyfriend made her feel wanted, secure. But her daughter? Her daughter was a piece of her soul. The idea that they were enemies, that one had to be chosen over the other, made her stomach turn.

Still, she kept quiet.

Each insult, each manipulative twist of words, wore Lin down. Her boyfriend would raise his voice if she tried to defend her daughter. He would accuse Lin of "always taking her side" and "undermining the relationship."

"She doesn't even live here anymore," he would argue. "Why are you letting someone who doesn't live here control our lives?"

And then came the guilt.

"You're a terrible mother," he would say. "You let her disrespect me. If you really loved me, you would've put me first."

Lin would sit on the couch, eyes downcast, lips sealed. She felt crushed under the weight of it all. The idea that she was a bad mother, that she had somehow failed her daughter or her partner, clawed at her self-esteem. She knew deep down that something was wrong, deeply wrong, but fear kept her silent. Fear of conflict. Fear of being alone. Fear of confirming that she had made a mistake by letting this man into their lives.

He insisted he was just "protecting" her.

"I'm trying to help you see things clearly," he would say, in a softer tone after every outburst. "I know it hurts, but you need to stop letting her manipulate you."

But that didn't feel like protection. It felt like erasure. It felt like he was trying to isolate her from the one person who truly had her back.

When her daughter would call and ask if something was wrong, Lin would fake a smile and say everything was fine. She didn't want to worry her. She didn't want to cause drama. So, she brushed it off, changed the subject, laughed a little too loudly.

Behind closed doors, though, she cried often. Sometimes quietly in the shower. Other times under the covers where no one could hear. The guilt was relentless. She missed her daughter but didn't know how to reach out without sparking another argument. Her boyfriend monitored her phone conversations now, always listening, always commenting afterward.

"She's brainwashing you," he would whisper. "She wants you all to herself. That's not love, Lin. That's obsession."

But the truth was clear to Lin in her heart: this was not about protection. It was about control. Little by little, her boyfriend was isolating her, not just from her daughter, but from her sense of self. He undermined her confidence, made her second-guess her instincts, and poisoned the sacred bond she had with her child.

There were days Lin would stare at the door, wondering what it would take to walk out. Other days she convinced herself that things were not that bad, that he was just struggling or misunderstood. But the emotional exhaustion was starting to show. She laughed less. She avoided calls. Her fire was burning out.

One evening, after a particularly harsh fight, Lin sat on the edge of her bed and finally allowed herself to admit what she had been too afraid to say aloud: *He's hurting me. Not with his fists, but with his words. And that hurt is just as deep.*

She picked up the phone and called her daughter.

"I need to talk to you," she said, voice shaking. "I think I've made some mistakes, and I don't know how to fix them."

There was silence on the line, then a soft, steady voice: "I'm here, Mom. I have always been here."

It wasn't the end, but it was a beginning.

Lin realized she didn't have to choose between love and family. Real love doesn't demand isolation. It doesn't insult or manipulate. It uplifts. And though the road ahead would be difficult, Lin had taken the first step, out of silence, out of guilt, and back toward the person she had always been: a mother. A protector. A woman worthy of respect.

# Santiago

Santiago had always hated the idea of women. He didn't understand them, didn't want to understand them, and certainly didn't think they had any real value beyond one biological function, reproduction. From a young age, his views were rigid and cruel. Unlike most boys who eventually matured into empathy or found respect through love or family, Santiago hardened. Where others saw potential partners or equals, he saw nuisances, distractions, or toys.

His attraction to women was purely physical, nothing more than the eyes pull of desire. Emotionally, mentally, and philosophically, he felt nothing but disdain. To him, femininity was a weakness, a hindrance to power and independence. He couldn't fathom why any man would cater to a woman's needs, emotions, or dreams. The very notion of caring about a woman's thoughts disgusted him. He prided himself on his detachment and control, his refusal to show affection, and his ability to dominate every interaction.

Santiago believed that women existed in society because nature had given them wombs. That was it. He didn't see them as thinkers, creators, or individuals. Just vessels. And so, in every relationship he ever had, he carried this belief like armor, ensuring no woman ever got too close or felt too comfortable. He thrived on belittling, mocking, and emotionally suffocating them.

His current relationship was no different. In fact, it was worse.

The woman he was with, Isabel, was kind, intelligent, and resilient. She had dreams, a career, and a spirit that once radiated confidence.

But Santiago had made it his mission to strip that away, piece by piece. He saw her strengths not as qualities to be admired or cherished, but as threats to his control. He couldn't stand the idea of her feeling good about herself unless it somehow benefited him.

In public, Santiago was a master of humiliation. He delighted in embarrassing Isabel whenever the opportunity arose. At dinners with friends, he would interrupt her mid-sentence, mocking her tone or correcting her facts even when she was right. If she dressed up, he would tell her she looked like she was trying too hard. If she dressed down, he would ask why she didn't care enough to look presentable. It was a constant game, a cruel cycle of lifting her up just enough to drop her harder each time.

What made Santiago particularly dangerous was his ability to mask this behavior as jokes or "honest opinions." Friends and acquaintances often brushed off his cruelty as sarcasm. They did not see the deep, lasting impact it was having on Isabel. They didn't hear the way he spoke to her in private. They didn't see the subtle sabotage he carried out day after day.

Isabel had tried to succeed despite him. She had earned a promotion at work, a significant one that had taken years of effort and late nights. When she told Santiago, his face had curled into a smirk. "That's cute," he said flatly. "Let's see how long that lasts before they realize you're not as good as you pretend to be." And then, the same week, he "accidentally" forgot to pick her up from an important client dinner she needed his support at, forcing her to arrive late and flustered. Afterward, he blamed her for not sending him a reminder.

He did things like this often, deliberately undermining her so she wouldn't rise above him, wouldn't gain confidence, wouldn't drift too far into a space where she might recognize her worth. He needed her to feel helpless, to need him, even as he treated her like nothing.

Despite it all, Isabel loved him. At least, she thought she did. Her love was tangled in the emotions, in a desperate hope that maybe she could change him, maybe he would see her, really see her, and one day appreciate all that she gave. But the deeper she fell into that illusion, the more Santiago tightened his grip. He used her love against her, crafting guilt-laced arguments that made her feel like she was always the problem. He painted himself as the victim of her "nagging," her "emotions," her "expectations."

Every attempt she made to leave him was thwarted by the invisible chains he had wrapped around her psyche. She would pack a bag, make a plan, even get as far as her friend's doorstep, but the moment he called, his voice suddenly soft, apologetic, promising change, her will collapsed. Not because she believed him, but because she couldn't bear the weight of starting over, of being alone, of thinking that maybe she had wasted all this time on someone who never genuinely loved her.

Santiago understood this dynamic. He didn't fear losing her. He didn't fear consequences. He knew that if he kept her unsure of herself, if he kept her questioning her worth, she would stay. And so, he continued the cycle.

He would hurt her, then charm her. He would insult her, then hold her. He would shame her, then apologize just enough to blur the lines between love and cruelty. He was not a man seeking redemption, nor did he see anything wrong with what he did. To him, power was the end goal, and women, especially Isabel, were tools to maintain that power.

This wasn't a relationship. It was a slow erosion of identity.

Isabel began to disappear beneath the weight of Santiago's toxicity. Her laughter became rarer, her posture more guarded. Her dreams, traveling, building something meaningful faded into the background. She second-guessed everything. Was she too sensitive? Too needy? Too ambitious?

Santiago made sure she believed she was.

And yet, a small part of her still hoped. Still remembered who she was before. That version of Isabel, the one with spark, with purpose, whispered to her in quiet moments. When Santiago was asleep, when she was alone, when she looked in the mirror and didn't recognize her glow. That whisper grew louder with each betrayal, each insult, each cold shoulder.

One day, perhaps, that whisper would become a roar.

But for now, Santiago remained in control. Sitting back, waiting for reactions, feeding off her pain like a leech. He didn't need her to be happy. He needed her to be his. Broken, compliant, afraid to leave.

In his mind, he had won.

But what he didn't understand, what he could never understand, was that love built on fear is fragile. Power built on cruelty is temporary. And no matter how tightly he gripped her, the human spirit, once pushed too far, finds a way to fight back.

Santiago was a man at war not just with women, but with anything he couldn't dominate. In his pursuit of control, he became a shell, emotionless, isolated, incapable of genuine connection. His hatred, his manipulation, his need to destroy what he couldn't understand, it didn't make him strong. It made him hollow.

And one day, when Isabel finds her strength, when she walks out for the last time and doesn't look back, Santiago will realize that all the power he thought he had was an illusion.

Because love cannot be forced.

And no one stays in a cage forever.

✝

# Layla

For years, Layla believed in the purity of their friendship. She and Marcus had been close since their early twenties, bonding over music, long talks, and a shared love for life's small joys. He was the steady presence in her life, the one who never missed a birthday, who brought soup when she was sick, who texted to check on her after tough dates. She often said he was her "safe place" the guy who expected nothing but gave so much. Or so she thought.

In their world, they were inseparable, sibling-like. But to Marcus, the friendship was a waiting room, a temporary space where he endured time, hoping she would one day see what he believed was obvious: that he was the one.

Each time Layla dated someone new, Marcus offered his thoughts, unsolicited and often scathing. "He's not on your level," he would say. "He talks too much about himself," or "He won't last a month." Layla brushed it off as protective concern. After all, she had her share of failed attempts at love, and Marcus had always been there to comfort her when things fell apart. What she didn't know was that each failed relationship only deepened the bitter seed Marcus had buried inside himself, a toxic mix of entitlement and rejection that quietly grew over the years.

Marcus never confessed outright. He would drop hints, send mixed signals, act moody when she talked about other men. But Layla, ever trusting, never read into it too deeply. She had made it clear early on that she saw him as a friend, a brother. And while Marcus said he understood, the truth was he never accepted it.

What Layla thought was kindness was, in many ways, a campaign. He tried to earn her love by being consistent, believing one day she would wake up and choose him. And when she didn't, his warmth started to curdle into resentment.

It started subtly, backhanded compliments, passive-aggressive remarks, silences that lasted longer than usual after she talked about her dates. Then came the commentary behind her back. To mutual friends, Marcus painted her as impossible to please, emotionally closed off, too proud, sassy, too picky. "She thinks she doesn't need anyone," he would say with a sad smile. "But she's gonna wake up one day and realize she's alone."

The words sounded like concern, but they were laced with malice. He wanted people to see her the way he had come to see her, not as someone strong and self-sufficient, but as broken, unlovable, and destined to fail without him. When Layla began focusing on herself, investing in her business, healing from past wounds, and finding happiness outside of romantic relationships, Marcus couldn't bear it. She was supposed to crumble without a man. She was supposed to, eventually, turn around and choose him.

But she didn't.

And instead of stepping back or moving on, Marcus dug in deeper, subtly sabotaging her. He would show up at events only to challenge her ideas, mock her choices, or dismiss her accomplishments in front of others. When she launched a successful project, he claimed it was luck. If she posted something inspiring online, he would text her with a critique, or worse, make fun of her behind her back. He became an emotional dumping ground, a person whose presence began to feel unpredictable, draining, and strangely hostile.

Still, Layla tried to make it work. She couldn't understand why someone who had been so supportive now seemed intent on jabbing her. She questioned herself, wondering if she was imagining it or being too sensitive. After all, wasn't Marcus her friend?

The final blow came not from something he said to her, but from what she overheard. At a small gathering, a friend confided in her that Marcus had been saying cruel things. That she was "damaged goods," that no man could "handle her," and that she would "die alone trying to prove she didn't need anyone. That she was bind to what has been in her face."

The words were a slap to her face.

In that moment, everything fell into place. The judgment, the criticism, the emotional coldness. She saw it clearly; Marcus hadn't been a friend. He had been a spectator to her life, waiting in the wings, and when she didn't perform the role, he wanted her to play, he turned on her. Not with honesty or distance, but with sabotage and growing disdain.

It broke her.

Not because she had lost someone she loved romantically, but because she had trusted him. She had confided in him, let him see her at her most vulnerable, allowed him into spaces and places of her life where she didn't let many. And he had used that access not to support her, but to quietly punish her for not choosing him.

She confronted him calmly, but firmly. She asked him why he had said those things. At first, he denied it. Then, when the lies couldn't stand anymore, he shifted the blame.

"I waited for years," he said. "I was always there. And you treated me like I was nothing."

Layla blinked. "I treated you like a friend. That's what you said you wanted."

"I lied," he snapped. "I thought maybe if I stayed long enough, you'd realize I was the one."

Her heart sank. All those years, every memory, every moment, twisted now under the weight of truth. What she thought was real friendship had been a transaction to him, one where he believed patience would eventually win her. And when it didn't, he sought to break her spirit instead.

After that day, she walked away. It hurt, deeply, but it also freed her. The illusion was gone, and with it, the constant confusion and guilt she had carried in his presence. She began to redefine her boundaries, to not surround herself with people who had a personal agenda.

Marcus faded into the background, left with his bitterness and regret. He had built his identity around a woman who never asked to be loved that way, and when she refused to bend, he broke the very thing he claimed to value, her friendship.

Layla, for her part, rose. She continued her journey, stronger, wiser, and more cautious with her trust. She didn't let the experience harden her, but it taught her something invaluable: that not all who stay by your side are there for the right reasons, and sometimes the most dangerous betrayal is the one that wears the mask of loyalty.

She no longer needed validation from anyone, least of all from someone who only loved the idea of her, not the reality. She didn't look back.

Some friendships aren't built on love. They are built on expectations, on silent demands, on conditional affection masked as support. And when those expectations go unmet, they rot from the inside.

Layla chose herself. And in doing so, she finally found the support she had always been searching for, not in a partner or a friendship, but in her own damn strength.

✝

*"Making yourself small so someone else can feel seen isn't noble,*
*it's crippling."*

✝

*"From one heart to another. I see you."*

✝

# Taylor

He was a serial cheater, and still, she stayed. When it came to women, he had no discipline, his lower impulses governed him. She was hurting, not just from his betrayals, but from the anger she carried toward herself for staying. No matter how many times he crossed the line, she forgave him.

She didn't want to look like a failure in the eyes of her friends and family. He made her believe it was her responsibility to hold the relationship together, to fix whatever was broken. Maybe, if she stayed long enough, he would finally see her, truly see her and devote himself to her. Maybe he'd stop disappearing on late-night business trips, start taking her out more, and stop acting like he was ashamed to be seen with her. Maybe he'd even show her some affection. Love. Care.

She couldn't understand how someone could build a life with another person while treating infidelity like a game. It felt reckless. Isolating. Dangerous.

She questioned whether she should keep waiting for him to change, but the truth was, she no longer had the emotional strength to leave. Her world had been built around him, and he knew it. He was confident she would never walk away.

So, she suffered quietly, night after night. She numbed the pain with food, silenced her cries, and pretended to be asleep when she heard him come home at 2 a.m. Almost every night, he retreated to the guest bedroom. And when she asked why, he turned the blame around, insisting it was out of courtesy, not wanting to wake her.

This was her marriage: a cycle of disrespect, dismissal, and emotional abandonment. She swallowed every lump in her throat, buried every insult, and let him do as he pleased. All for the sake of avoiding another argument. All in the hope that one day, he would recognize the good wife she tried so hard to be.

✝

# Cat

Once upon a time, Cat believed in love. She believed in fairytale endings, in forever promises, in gentle hands and honest eyes. But time, and man after man, taught her a different lesson. Betrayal, manipulation, infidelity, and lies slowly chipped away at the soft woman she once was, until all that remained was a hardened version of her former self. The girl who used to cry over heartbreaks became a woman who laughed at vulnerability. The woman who used to give endlessly had learned to take. And take she did, unapologetically.

After one particularly devastating breakup, Cat snapped. Something inside her said fuck it, and then reassembled, not as something fragile, but something sharp. Something lethal. She stopped seeking love and started seeking power, not the kind found in boardrooms or corner offices, but the kind that lived in glances, desires, and fantasies. The kind that men could not help but fall for. She became a savage, not by choice at first, but for survival.

Every wound she had ever endured transformed into a weapon. Her heartbreaks were blades. Her disappointments, shields. The tears she once cried had dried into bullets. She stopped wearing her heart on her sleeve and instead dressed her body like armor, tight dresses, heels that clicked like war drums, eyes lined in sharp defiance. She became irresistible, not only because of her beauty, which was undeniable, but because of the energy she exuded. Controlled chaos. Sensual destruction. Men didn't just want her. They *worshipped* her.

Cat weaponized her sexuality like a master tactician. Every glance, every whisper, every soft touch was calculated. She studied the way men moved, what made them tick, what made them crumble. Her downtime was no longer for daydreaming about love or scrolling through old texts. She used it to sculpt her body, learn new tricks, and refine her methods. Gym by day, seductress by night. Her curves weren't just attractive, they were a trap. A beautiful, inescapable snare that men willingly walked into.

At first, her friends thought it was just a phase, the bitter reaction of a broken woman. "She's just hurt," they would say, shaking their heads. "She'll come back around." But Cat never came back. In fact, she leaned in harder, indulged deeper. What started as an emotional defense mechanism soon became a lifestyle. A thrill. A game. A means of survival and expression. Men became pawns. If one so much as said "hello" in a suggestive tone, he became her next target. Some she used for money. Others for status. A few just for sport.

The more she played the game, the more she perfected her role. Some men, the bold ones, even whispered it before she had to ask: "Use me." And she did, without blinking. Without guilt. Without remorse. To the world, Cat was unstoppable. Men adored her, women envied her. She turned heads everywhere she went, not just because of her beauty, but because she moved like a woman who knew her power. She *owned* the room.

But not everything glittered inside her like it did on the outside.

Despite her cold exterior, there were nights quiet, private ones, when the noise of her lifestyle faded, and silence roared louder than any party ever could. On those nights, as she lay alone in the king-sized bed she rarely shared twice with the same man, she felt it, the ache. A low, constant yearning in the depths of her soul. Not for a particular man. Not for the past. But for *herself,* the version of her that used to dream, to trust, to love. That version felt so far gone now, a distant memory blurred by champagne, perfumes, and bodies that never stayed.

Cat's principles, once clearly defined, were now in a permanent state of negotiation. She compromised often, not just her standards, but her essence. Each time she brushed it off, telling herself she was just too busy, too evolved, too far gone. But the truth lingered, unspoken but ever-present: she missed believing in something pure. Something sacred.

Still, she kept going.

She told herself the world didn't deserve the soft parts of her. She convinced herself that every man, no matter how good he seemed, would eventually hurt her. That even if Prince Charming did exist, she wouldn't be able to trust him anyway. So why bother?

Then, it happened.

She met someone different. He didn't chase. He didn't flirt with the same reckless abandon. He listened. He looked at her like she was more than a trophy. He spoke to the parts of her she had buried, the real parts. The forgotten parts. For a brief moment, she felt something stir within her. A possibility. A glimpse of what she might have had in another life, a life where she wasn't a jaded, guarded, savage.

But she shut it down.

"This is how it starts," she warned herself. "They charm you. They draw you in. Then they destroy you."

She ghosted him before he had the chance to try. She returned to the nightclubs, the penthouses, the fleeting pleasures. It was easier that way. Safer. Cleaner.

She clung to the lifestyle, even as it frayed the edges of her soul. The material comforts it brought, the designer clothes, the lavish vacations, the attention, became her new form of affection. A twisted replacement for emotional intimacy. She called it "living." Some days it even felt like freedom. Other days, it felt like a gilded cage.

There were moments when she would catch her reflection, not in the mirror, but in the expressions of the men she used. She saw the same pain in their eyes that she once carried. She saw longing. Confusion. Emptiness. It didn't always make her feel powerful. Sometimes it just reminded her of how far she had fallen from who she used to be.

But turning back wasn't an option.

Healing would require slowing down. Sitting with herself. Peeling back layers. Facing pain. And that, she wasn't ready for. Or she didn't believe she deserved it. Either way, she stayed in motion, because motion distracted her from the truth.

She knew she could never trust again. Not fully. Not enough to open her heart and risk it all. So, she played her role like a reality show superstar, dramatic, dazzling, untouchable. She lived like she was always on camera, like the world was watching and waiting to see what she would do next.

And in a way, it was.

To many, Cat was an icon, a symbol of feminine vengeance, of beauty sharpened into a blade. But beneath the makeup, beneath the curated perfection, beneath the persona, was a woman still hurting. A woman whose power was real, but whose pain was deeper. A woman who had rewritten the rules of love but couldn't forget how it once felt to follow them.

Cat wasn't lost. She was *transformed.* But transformation always comes at a cost. And every night, as she slid between expensive sheets alone, she paid a little more.

She didn't cry anymore. She didn't hope. But somewhere, deep in the quiet of her soul, the girl she used to be still whispered. Not loud enough to change her. But just loud enough to remind her that she was still in there, waiting.

Waiting for the day when savage wasn't her only survival mode.

# Fin

## His Baggage, Blessing, and Boundaries of a Toxic Relationship

Fin wasn't the kind of man who liked to make waves. A quiet, thoughtful presence in most rooms, he had always been more inclined to listen than speak. But silence, as he would later come to learn, can be both a sanctuary and prison. His story is one of survival, not the dramatic kind with sirens and headlines, but the slow, subtle, suffocating kind. The kind that begins with a sigh and ends, if one is lucky, with a deep breath of freedom.

Fin carried more than he showed. Like most people, he had his share of emotional baggage, though he had long convinced himself he was managing it. In truth, he had simply become accustomed to its weight. Much of it stemmed from his childhood. His father was distant, emotionally unavailable, and quick to judge. His mother, though loving, was burdened herself, lost in her own anxieties and depression. Fin learned early that love was conditional, often transactional, and that to be seen, he had to perform, be helpful, agreeable, and non-confrontational.

So, he grew into a man who rarely said "no," who excused harmful behavior and internalized blame. He told himself he was "mature" for avoiding conflict, when in reality, he feared rejection. Every friendship, job, and relationship he entered came with this invisible luggage, old thoughts whispering, *"You are only lovable if you are useful. You are responsible for everyone's feelings but your own."*

When Fin met Clara, she seemed like a star. Vibrant, magnetic, and emotionally expressive, she pulled Fin into her orbit with ease. At first, she praised his calmness, his ability to "understand her better than anyone." But slowly, the tone shifted.

The praise became expectation. Understanding became an obligation. Clara's love came with rules that kept changing. She would explode at minor slights, then cry and beg for forgiveness. Fin, accustomed to unstable affection, interpreted her volatility as passion. He thought If *I can just be better, more attentive, more patient... she'll be happy. She'll love me consistently.* But her happiness was a moving target, and Fin was always adjusting himself to chase it.

He didn't realize it, but his baggage had found a familiar home.

Despite everything, Fin had a blessing: his empathy. It was both his curse and his gift, and learning the difference would become the cornerstone of his transformation. He had an extraordinary ability to feel what others were feeling, to listen deeply and respond with compassion. That's what drew Clara in. That's also what kept him trapped until he learned to redirect that compassion inward.

There was a pivotal night when Clara accused Fin of deliberately ignoring her texts, though he had simply been in a work meeting. The fight escalated quickly. She screamed, cried, accused him of being manipulative and cold. As usual, Fin apologized. He didn't believe he had done anything wrong, but he apologized to de-escalate, to smooth things over. He tried to be mindful of how anger felt, but sometimes fatigue took over.

He questioned himself after she stormed out. His eyes were tired. His posture slumped. And for the first time in years, he asked himself: *What about me?*

That question was the beginning of everything. He began asking himself questions and being real with the answers. He couldn't see himself finding a therapist, but he found ways to get support from nature and meeting new friends. And slowly, he began to see that showing love and empathy must not come at the cost of self-respect. He realized his blessing was not just his ability to feel for others but also his ability to grow, to unlearn, to reclaim.

He remembered small pieces of himself he had long buried: his love for the arts, the way he used to write poetry, his curiosity about sailing. Clara had always dismissed those interests as "a waste of time," and Fin had agreed too quickly. But now, he began to reclaim them, not for validation, but for joy.

His blessing was not just who he was, but who he could become when he started loving himself the way he loved others.

With growth came confrontation. Fin began to learn about boundaries, not as walls to push people away, but as gates to protect what was reserved within. He learned that "no" was a complete sentence. He learned that love without respect is not love at all, but dependency wrapped in barbed wire.

When he started setting boundaries with Clara, the fallout was immediate. She accused him of changing, of becoming selfish, of "giving up on them." But Fin, though still hurting, stood his ground. He told her he could no longer be in a relationship that demanded he erase himself. He didn't blame her; he simply chose himself.

It wasn't easy. Leaving someone you love, even when it is toxic, can feel like tearing your soul in two. He mourned not just the relationship, but the dreams he had pinned his hopes on. He mourned the version of himself who had tried so hard to make it work. But in mourning, there was also release.

Boundaries gave Fin breathing room, and with air came clarity. He saw how much of his identity had been shaped by fear, fear of abandonment, of not being enough, of being "too much." And now, with space to grow, he started becoming whole.

He didn't demonize Clara, nor did he excuse her. He simply accepted that some people bring lessons, not lifetimes.

Healing didn't come all at once. There were days Fin still doubted himself. Days when he replayed arguments in his mind, wondering if he had done more harm than he thought. But with time, the noise grew quieter, and his inner voice, once drowned out, grew stronger.

He developed new routines. Morning walks. Coffee in silence. Music with no agenda. He made new friends, ones who respected his boundaries and encouraged his growth. He revisited therapy, not because he was crazy, but because he was worth the effort of staying whole.

He no longer needed chaos to feel alive. Peace, he discovered, was not boring; it was revolutionary.

Fin's story isn't uncommon, though it is rarely told. Men in toxic relationships often go unrecognized, especially those who are gentle, giving, and emotionally intelligent. Society tells them to "man up," to be stoic, to never admit pain. But Fin's strength was not in hiding his strength was in confronting, feeling, and changing.

His baggage didn't disappear, but he learned to carry it with awareness. He unpacked what wasn't his to carry and repacked only what served his growth.

His blessing was never lost, only misdirected. Now, it flowed not just outward, but inward.

His boundaries were his liberation. They didn't make him hard; they made him clear-minded.

Fin eventually shared his story not loudly, not dramatically, but honestly. He spoke at a local men's group about emotional abuse and recovery. He volunteered for a support line. He drafted essays. He wasn't looking for applause. He just wanted someone else, another quiet man sitting in the corner, to know they were not alone.

In every room he entered, Fin still listened. But now, when he spoke, his voice did not shake. He no longer performed for affection. He no longer begged to be seen. He stood in his truth, imperfect but free.

Fin's life became a quiet rebellion against everything that once told him to size down.

He didn't just survive toxic love. He transformed through it.

He became his own sanctuary.

✝

# Vonic

He was gifted with words smooth, eloquent, magnetic. Words were all he had, but he was never a man of his word. He broke her heart repeatedly, lied with ease, set her up for failure, only to turn around and promise her the world. Like a Grammy-winning songwriter, he poured his heart out in verses that sounded sincere, telling her he couldn't live without her just to reel her back in.

He was strategic. He studied her, knew her passion for love, her honest vulnerability, and her open-hearted nature. Her transparency became his playground, a space where he could perform tricks and illusions, always keeping her wasting time inside a one-way maze. And she ran, in and out of his life because of how he treated her.

Each time she returned, it was with the hope that he had changed, that he would finally learn how to treat her with respect and dignity. She believed in the potential of their love and was willing to stay the course, waiting for him to rise to it. Somewhere along the way, she convinced herself it was her fault, so she dimmed her own light, made herself smaller so he could shine.

She was tired of the dating scene. All she wanted was something real. So, she started keeping her heart more guarded, more private, hoping it would protect her from being used. At 40, she decided to give love one last real try. That is when she met him.

He seemed decent at first, a bit arrogant and loud, not exactly her type, but she overlooked that in the name of connection. They dated for a year, broke up, and then reconciled. She forgave him. Then came another year, more breakups, more bizarre behavior. Again, she forgave. She always forgave.

But the final breakup hit differently. She felt drained, overwhelmed, and chose to end it for good. That's when he returned, begging, pleading, addicted to the chase, it seemed. The thrill wasn't in loving her; it was in losing her and pulling her back in again. But this time, she was done. She didn't respond. She had finally seen through the cycle.

He came on strong, day and night, insisting he couldn't live without her, though his actions said otherwise. She didn't want grand speeches anymore. She wanted sacrifice. Follow-through. Proof that his words held weight. He always said the right things, but never did the right things.

She turned down his advances, one by one, knowing she deserved more. Eventually, she agreed to meet for closure, ready to release the anger and sadness. That is when he sensed she was truly over it, and he pulled out every trick in his playbook. He begged for forgiveness, declared his love, even offered to pay off a major bill, no strings attached as a gesture of remorse.

She didn't believe him. She had heard it all before. But this time, she responded differently. She detached her emotions and thought clearly. She spoke his language, money. Normally, she would have declined. But she accepted, just to see if he meant it.

The moment she did, he backpedaled. He accused her of being manipulative, greedy, of trying to take advantage of "poor little him." He called the offer "ridiculous" and "financially reckless." Then he showed her his bank account not to prove he couldn't, but to assert that he wouldn't. He feared she would leave after he followed through as if love were a transaction.

He kept flipping the narrative, gaslighting her, alternating between claims of love and cries of victimhood. Days later, still pushing for reconciliation, he danced around the topic of the bill again. When she pressed him, he offered to pay in monthly installments, a compromise, that she refused.

She looked him in the eyes and said:

*"The payoff you offered, I'll just count it as one more thing you didn't follow through on."*

This time, she wanted accountability. Not flowers. Not promises. Just a tangible act that said he was willing to *fight* for her.

What he didn't know was that she had way more than what he offered to payoff in her own account. She could have paid off that $22,139.69 bill herself ten times over. But it was never about the money.

It was about truth. Integrity. Action. And she had finally realized, he had none of it.

His games had grown old. His voice no longer moved her. And in that moment, she stopped waiting to be loved by someone incapable of loving her right. She walked, like a country song. "Head up and not a frown, but she did glance back to see a man had fallen down."

✝

# Ezekiel

They were a young couple, seemingly in sync, occasionally laughing over coffee or walking hand-in-hand through crowded streets. But something was off kilter in the way his shoulders slumped when she spoke too loudly, or the way he hesitated before answering her in front of others, searching her face for signals of approval or scorn. It wasn't love that held them together. It was something quieter, more tragic: his hope that things could be better, and her certainty that they never would be.

She taunted him often, and never with warmth. There was a sharpness in her words that sliced just enough to bleed but not enough to scar visibly. At dinners with friends or casual meetups, she found humor in tearing him down. She would mock the way he ate, too slow, too fast, too deliberate, as if his every movement was performance art to be ridiculed. His accent, shaped by childhood summers with his grandparents, became the punchline of her impersonations. And when he mentioned, even shyly, that he called his mother every day, she rolled her eyes and sighed dramatically, saying things like, *"You are not ten anymore. Grow up."*

What he hoped would be endearing, his loyalty to family, his soft heart, was ammunition in her arsenal. The more vulnerable he became, the more she twisted the knife.

Still, he stayed. Not because he didn't see what was happening, but because he kept hoping she had come around. That she was just hurting in ways she could not articulate. That, if he was patient enough, gentle enough, she would finally see him, not as a man to fix or mock, but as a partner. Someone worth meeting halfway.

But kindness was never enough.

Behind his back, she told her friends stories painted with cruel exaggeration. She would laugh about how he had wept during a fight, how he had confessed how much he loved her, how he had pleaded with her not to leave. She made it sound pathetic. *"He acts like I'm the last woman on Earth,"* she would say between sips of wine. *"Honestly, it's sad. I could leave tomorrow, and he would probably write me a novel begging me back."*

Her friends would laugh, not always because they agreed, but because they didn't know what else to do. Her cruelty had a charisma to it, a kind of biting wit that was easier to laugh at than challenge. And so, the stories continued: she was the prize, he was the fool.

What she did not tell them, what she wouldn't admit even to herself, was that he was never truly her type. From the beginning, she had been drawn to more brash, unattainable men: people who didn't linger, who didn't love too deeply, who did not make her question her own reflection. He was different, so open-hearted, so ready to build something stable, that it disarmed her. And in time, what had first intrigued her began to irritate her. His consistency felt suffocating. His emotional availability made her feel exposed. And rather than confront her own discomfort, she resented him for it.

That resentment festered. It transformed into contempt, expressed not through screaming matches or dramatic exits, but through a thousand small humiliations. She knew how to push his buttons. Make him beg when he feared loosing her, when to drop the name of an ex who had texted her, how to mention a coworker's flirtation in casual conversation, or how to suggest that she could "do better" without actually saying the words. It was all calculated. She wanted him to feel insecure. To believe that he was lucky she hadn't left yet. That he had to keep earning her presence.

And he tried. My god, did he try. He changed the way he dressed because she told him his style was dated. He picked up cooking because she once joked that he was helpless in the kitchen. He cut off a friend she didn't like, even though he missed the camaraderie. He worked longer hours, bought her thoughtful gifts, remembered the anniversaries of moments she herself had forgotten. His love was relentless, and her appreciation was fleeting, if it ever existed at all.

No matter what he did, it was never enough.

When he got a promotion at work, something he had worked toward for years, he told her over dinner with a quiet, hopeful smile. She nodded without looking up from her phone and said, *"That's nice. You know, Jared from accounting is already a VP, and he's younger than you."*

That night, he lay in bed beside her, eyes open in the dark, replaying the moment in his head. For this first time he was angry, he rarely allowed himself that, because he couldn't understand what he had done wrong. Was it too much to want her to be proud of him?

She meanwhile, never stopped playing her games. She would wear perfume she knew reminded him of their first date, then casually mention another man's compliment on it later that day. She would disappear for hours without explanation, then act insulted when he asked where she had been. When he gave her space, she accused him of detachment. When he showed emotion, she called him needy.

He was in a loop to loop of confusion and despair. He kept thinking that if he could just find the right way to love her. more softly, more fiercely, more completely, he asked himself, "what could he do that would shift her behavior? Would She see him?"

But she never did.

And deep down, he began to realize she never would. She did not want to see him, because truly seeing him would mean confronting her own inability to love someone so openheartedly. And that scared her more than she would ever admit.

He wasn't perfect, of course. He had his flaws, insecurities that ran deep, moments of self-doubt that made him retreat rather than confront. But he had never stopped trying. He didn't want much: just peace, kindness, someone to come home to who didn't see his vulnerability as a weakness.

And yet, every attempt he made to build that kind of life with her was met with sabotage. Her laughter at his tears, her coldness in the face of his tenderness, her calculated jealousy, all of it chipped away at the man he had once been.

He started speaking less, retreating into himself, afraid that anything he said might become the next punchline in her stories. His friends noticed. They asked if everything was okay. He always smiled and said yes because he was ashamed. Ashamed that he had allowed himself to be disrespected in this way, embarrassed that he still loved someone who treated him like he was disposable.

Eventually, something in him began to ask more questions not in a dramatic, explosive way, but quietly, like a tide turning. One morning, she mocked him for crying during a movie. He didn't respond. He just looked at her, not with anger, but with an eerie kind of clarity. It was the look of a man who had finally understood that the love he was giving would never be returned. That staying meant shrinking. That peace would never come from someone who fed on his uncertainty.

That night, for the first time, he didn't call her to say goodnight. He didn't text to ask where she was. He sat alone, breathing in silence. And in that stillness, he began to imagine a life without her, a life not defined by emotional landmines and humiliations.

He took his time. Untangling love from habit, devotion from self-betrayal. But he had taken the first step.

And she? She would go on telling stories, casting herself as the victim or the star, depending on the audience. But a part of her would know, somewhere deep beneath the bravado, that she had once been loved by someone who gave her everything.

And that she had thrown it away.

# O's Quiet Grief and Hard-Won Freedom

Grief has many faces. Sometimes it's loud, full of sobs and shattered glass. Sometimes it is a quiet weight that sits behind your eyes, in your chest, in your bones. For her, it was the latter. A silent, private ache that followed her like a shadow no one else could see. Her grief was not for someone who had died, but for someone she had finally let go of love that had poisoned her spirit, a relationship that had eroded the foundations of who she was.

There was a loneliness in that kind of grief. A kind that could not be easily explained to others without opening wounds she wasn't ready to show. People often didn't understand why leaving someone could hurt just as much, sometimes more than being left. But she knew. She felt it in the small moments, in the quiet hum of a morning where his presence was no longer part of the routine, in the silence of a night without his chaos, without the phone calls, without the battles.

And there was so much work to do inside and out. Her life had to be pieced back together, and it wasn't about changing her address or updating her phone number. It was about rebuilding her self-worth, redefining her peace, and reclaiming her identity. Every day she had to make the decision again: to stay away, to stay gone, to stay strong. And though she was moving forward, that didn't mean the path was smooth.

There were plenty of moments when she longed to go back not because she missed him, not exactly. But because the chaos, as destructive as it was, had become familiar. And familiarity can be seductive. In the chaos, there had been a warped sense of predictability. She knew how to navigate his moods, how to avoid his triggers, how to read between the lines of his silence. And when you spend enough time learning how to survive in dysfunction, it starts to feel like home.

There were nights when she sat alone and wondered if she had overreacted. If he *had* meant well but just didn't know how to love her right. Those were the dangerous hours, the ones where the mind starts playing tricks, rewriting history with gentler hands. She would think back on the good days, the charming words, the smiles that made her heart soften. She would recall the way he had once held her hand with a kind of desperate tenderness that made her believe, even if just for a moment, that he genuinely cared.

But then she would remember the other side the coldness, the manipulation, the way kindness always came with strings attached. The way he apologized only when it suited him, how he weaponized guilt, how he always managed to twist her feelings until she was the one saying sorry. She remembered the emotional rollercoaster he kept her on, how he would build her up just to push her down again, and how every promise he made came wrapped in hope but unraveled into heartbreak.

The more he reached out, the more clearly, she saw the pattern. Every time he called, he said all the right things. He spoke with a softness she had once begged for. He swore he had changed. He promised to treat her better; to finally become the man she had needed him to be. He painted a picture of a different future filled with kindness, stability, love. But she had learned to see the truth behind his words. He didn't want to change for her; he wanted her to come back so he wouldn't have to.

And in those moments, she was proud of herself, even if it came with pain. Proud for recognizing manipulation disguised as affection. Proud for not folding under the weight of loneliness. Proud for choosing herself, even though that choice was isolating and exhausting. Because the truth was, he only ever offered her the basics love on his terms, safety if she did not provoke him, peace only if she kept quiet. And even that was unstable.

His world had always been unsafe. It was unpredictable and filled with emotional drama. She never knew what version of him she would wake up to the sweet talker, the brooding victim, or the angry aggressor. She had spent too much time tiptoeing around his moods, twisting herself to fit whatever shape he needed in the moment. But no more. She was learning to take up space again.

Still, his absence lingered. Not in the way you miss someone's presence, but in the way a room still smells like smoke long after the fire's been put out. It was like an overpowering odor that clung to her clothes, her memories, her habits. She would flinch at the sound of a raised voice, second-guess herself before speaking, and apologize reflexively. His ghost was in those reactions, in the trauma that lived in her system.

And deep down, she knew his silence was never permanent. He always pulled back before a storm. Disappearing was part of his pattern. He would retreat just long enough to make her question everything, just long enough for her guard to come down. And then he would come back stronger, louder, sweeter. He would say just enough to get her to respond. And once she did, once he saw a crack in the wall she had built, he would start prying it open with promises, memories, guilt.

But this time, she didn't respond.

She learned that silence could be a weapon too, a powerful, healing one. She learned that not every message needed a reply, that not every plea was sincere. She saw how much of her energy she had wasted trying to fix someone who didn't want to grow and trying to make someone love her the way she deserved. And now, she was redirecting that energy inward.

She was reconnecting with parts of herself she had buried. The part that used to laugh without restraint. The part that dreamed. The part that felt joy without fear that it would be taken away. She was remembering what it meant to be at peace not the fragile peace that came from avoiding conflict, but the deep, grounded peace that comes from knowing you are safe, even if you are alone.

She found comfort in her solitude. Not always, and not easily. But there were moments sunlit mornings with coffee in hand, evenings wrapped in a cozy blanket that reminded her healing was possible. That life didn't have to be chaotic to be meaningful. That love should not come at the cost of her sanity or her spirit.

Her grief stayed, of course. Healing isn't linear. Some days the ache was sharper than others. Some days she still missed what could have been. But she no longer missed *him*. She missed the version of love she had hoped for, not the one she received. And that distinction made all the difference.

In time, the silence between them stopped feeling like tension and started feeling like freedom. She stopped checking her phone. Stopped expecting apologies. Stopped needing his validation to feel whole. The distance became peace, a boundary, not a punishment.

And slowly, she began to forgive herself. For staying as long as she did. For trying so hard to make it work. For all the ways she had silenced her own needs in the name of love. Because now she understood leaving wasn't the easy way out. It was the bravest thing she had ever done.

Her grief was a lonely one. But in that loneliness, she found truth. She found clarity. She found a woman in herself who one day was willing to trust love again.

*"Don't worry about the sounds of the storm, focus on its pattern."*

✝

"You know, I want you to understand something they're not gonna say sorry. They're not gonna change. They are not coming back as a better version. So, stop standing in the Fxxxx ashes like the fire wasn't real. Closure doesn't come in a text it doesn't come in that one last phone call, it doesn't come in the apology they might give if they ever grow up. It comes the second you realize that love without respect is nothing nada, zero. That effort without consistency is manipulation, that history without accountability is dead weight. Closure comes when you stop pumping CPR into a connection that's been emotionally rotting for months and finally say to yourself "I deserve more than the Fxxxx crumbs I kept calling a meal." You gave them chances, you gave them grace, you gave them the most rare loyal, version of you and they still gambled like it was nothing, so you know what? Close the book. Not gently, not tearfully. Slam it shut like the ending was never even worth the pages. Closure is not about forgiving them. It's about finally choosing you without the need for validation, without the craving you have for revenge, without the hope they'll ever become who you wanted them to be. They won't. But you will and from now on, from now on, you just don't turn the pages you burn the whole Fxxxx book."

– IG: Dominic. Micheal. Project 24